# BARREN

## Elizabeth Miceli

*To Grandma Miceli, for passing down your love of reading to me.*
*I miss you.*

# BARREN

Elizabeth Miceli

# Prologue

*Winter*

There's not a lot that I remember about that night. It's all a blur between the red cup in my hand and the morning … but I do remember this December night as being one of the turning points in my life. I was just starting to feel self-confident because I was finally at goal weight. All that running had finally paid off, and I was one hundred forty pounds, which, for me, was like one hundred ten for most girls, because (let's be honest) I wasn't small. I was pretty tall, had a big butt, strong legs, and broad shoulders from all that working out. The problem was I didn't know how to eat. Food controlled me in a way that people couldn't. It was my vice, my nemesis, and at times, my only love.

After a much-needed intervention from my primary care doctor last year, I'd decided enough was enough, and I lost forty-five pounds by eating right, taking a diet pill, and working out at the YMCA. The only problem was, no matter how much weight I lost, I was never happy with myself. I never felt skinny enough, and I always felt worthless.

When I stepped into the party that night in my red Jimmy Choos, I had a mission: I was getting fucked up, and I was hooking up with someone. I knew that that would make me feel better, and I just wanted to forget. I wanted to forget everything.

I knew the guy I wanted to do all of this with, too. Devan Turner. We worked together at a restaurant downtown, and ever since the day I first saw him I wanted him. Devan came off very shy and sweet, but he also had a dangerous side. When I talked to him, I felt badass, because he was twenty, was the bartender at the restaurant, was weirdly good at snowboarding, had tattoos on every surface of his skin, had an earring, always had access to the best parties, and was definitely not a virgin. Whenever he texted me, I didn't feel like my old, fat self anymore. I felt like a girl who was finally attractive enough to get with an older, sexier, more experienced guy. I was worthy.

I started drinking at around ten. Boys handed me

alcohol, touching my waist as they slipped just "a little bit more" vodka into my red plastic cup. It went down hard, burning the back of my throat. But that pain felt like victory to me. Pain was better than feeling nothing.

When I finished my fourth cup, I knew I might have hit the bottle a little too quickly. My words were slurring, my body trembling, and when Devan came into my view, I was seeing four of him at once.

"Devan!" His arms came around me and held on tight. As he let go, my body shifted to one side, and I almost fell. Thankfully, he steadied me with ease. He took the cup in my hand and took a sip, shaking his head approvingly.

"You're going hard there, beautiful," he joked.

"Drinking isn't the only time I go hard," I slurred. His eyes came down to mine and held. It was like I couldn't move, couldn't breathe when he was staring at me that way. I looked up at him and his gorgeous red hair. I took a fistful of it in my hands and let my fingertips linger on his skin.

My right hand grabbed his arm, and I led him upstairs. I stumbled, but his hands held strong to my waist. He was so much taller, bigger, than me. He made me feel like a little girl.

The door closed behind me as he kissed me. It was rushed and very forward … but I wanted it. And I didn't want him to stop.

"Baby … " His words tickled my left earlobe as he lifted my dress over my head. All I had on now were heels and a thong. Gently, he led me to the bed in the corner of the room. I held on to his shoulders as he glided my clothes off of my body.

I had never been so turned on in my life. I was a virgin, and he was taking that from me tonight. Tonight … I was skinny, and a size four, and all of those years of me being fat would slip away. Unlike back then, I would be wanted. I would be needed. I would get him turned on.

My stomach turned as he touched me from my shoulders to my breasts, and then to my belly button. His hands were sure, experienced. Moisture pooled between my legs as he kissed and caressed me. Devan knew just how to make me feel good, and it made me want to have sex with him all the more. I wondered what else he could make me feel.

"Either you're really tight, or you're a virgin." He laughed as one finger gently glided inside me.

The look of shock on my face made him laugh as he took off his boxer briefs. He was much larger than any boy I'd ever been with. And he was definitely hard and ready for me.

"I … " He pulled my body up to his and kissed me.

"I'm a v—" My lips were betraying me. It was so hard to get the words out.

"Virgin?" His hands instantly stopped moving, frozen on my stomach. "You could have fucking told me." He was getting up now, pacing and looking for his shirt in the dark room.

"I … " Tears filled my eyes. I had never wanted someone so much, and he was now pushing me away …

"I can't do this with you. You're clingy enough. I don't need your virginal attachments to me." He pulled his boxers up over his calves, then thighs, and did the same with his jeans. In a minute, he was gone. And I was naked and alone.

My friends Marie and Lindsey saw me in the hallway, and I disregarded them, heading straight for the bathroom. I knew what would make me feel better; I knew what I had to do. I turned on the sink so the water was flowing hard. I put my index finger and middle finger together and stuck them under the flowing water. I left the water running as I knelt down on the cold tile beside the toilet.

I pushed my tears off my face with my arm and took a strong, deep breath. I kept my mouth open and stuck my wet fingers inside my mouth, pushing them far enough to massage the back of my throat. Calories poured from my mouth, and for just a few seconds I was soaring.

It was like an orgasm. It made my toes curl and my body numb. Just like Devan touching me, purging made me feel content, wanted, loved. It made me feel like I had control over something in my life.

I wiped my mouth with a piece of toilet paper and took a deep breath, then threw it in the toilet and flushed. I flushed away Devan. I flushed away the sorrow. I flushed away the night.

# Chapter One

*September of the Following Year*

R idgefield Senior High School is one of the nicest-looking schools in the whole state of Rhode Island. Our state test scores are high, our SAT scores are even higher, and the whole town is crawling with overpaid, upper-middle-class white people. At Ridgefield, most of the students graduate with high honors and go on to higher levels of education.

I've lived in Ridgefield my whole life, and yet I was dreading the first day of senior year. I had to admit, I did look good, though. My black jeans fit me like a glove, sucking my legs in nicely. On top, I was rocking a vintage shirt of my mother's that I'd fallen in love with. It was lacey and black and form fitting, of course.

It left just an inch of my pale stomach exposed.

Now, I haven't really described my appearance to you, have I? Well, my mother calls me "Casper" … Yes, like the ghost. But, to make my paleness even weirder, I have jet-black hair in thick banana curls. I straighten it often, but on the first day of school I liked to show my true colors. Tight jeans, big earrings, crazy curls. Check. Check. Check.

I wouldn't call myself beautiful, especially not while standing around my group of girlfriends. Out of all of them, I'm totally the ugliest. But I'm not ugly in general. I'm just different-looking. The big ass, the curves, the style. It's something to get used to.

I walked toward the first-floor hallway, where all my friends were sitting in a congregation on the benches and floor. Everyone's location was very typical. My best friend, Clare, was on a bench, leaning on my other friend's Marie and Lindsey, who lived in my neighborhood. Cam, Lindsey's fuck buddy, was spotted next to Lindsey and his hand was inching up her thigh. Katie and Jen were sprawled out on the floor. Katie was braiding Jen's hair. Cam, Lindsey, Marie, Katie, and Jen were pretty cool people, but they weren't as close as Clare and I were.

"Stacey!" Clare jumped up and gave me a big hug. She was wearing jean shorts, a plain blue tank top, and her cowboy boots. This outfit described Clare. She rarely tried to impress anybody, hardly wore makeup, and almost never had to style her gorgeous blond locks like I did. She was very natural and carefree. She was an actress in the drama club—and I think she knew how great she was. Confidence spilled out of her. She didn't have to pretend.

"There's my boy," I said, laughing. We always joked that if we were in a relationship she'd be the boy and I'd be the girl because I was the emotional and sensitive one, and she didn't give a shit about anything. She had high self-esteem, and I hated my body. She was a C student, and I was planning on taking an AP class. She was gorgeous, and I was in her shadow.

"Well, your boy actually put on makeup today!" She stuck her face an inch from mine so I could examine her work. I had taught her to put on makeup hundreds of times, explained the way it works, the order you had to put things on, and she still struggled to cover up her pimples, and put on mascara. No matter how many productions she was in, she never got used to the idea of dressing up. All of her acting friends always made fun of her. Her understudy usually ended up applying her makeup for shows. Literally everyone had tried to help her, but it just wasn't her. She loved herself without makeup.

"Close," I said, laughing and taking her hand. "Come with me. I have my makeup bag in my purse."

She grabbed her jean jacket and backpack, said good-bye to our group of friends, and went straight to the bathroom.

I positioned her on the ground in front of me and took out my makeup bag. I applied concealer under her eyes and on a few of her pimples. "What would I do without you?" she said.

I couldn't help but wonder what it would be like if I wasn't here. It would be a lot easier if I didn't have to go to school, desperately try to lose weight, and figure my life out. But when I thought of my mother's face and what her reaction would be to my suicide—I pushed the thoughts away and laughed it off.

"I have no idea," I said, putting away the concealer and taking out the bronzer.

"Are you nervous?" Clare asked me, looking up at me with those big green eyes. It was as if she knew that I had just been thinking about killing myself. She could always tell.

"Yeah, I guess," I said, trying to downplay my anxiety.

"Come on! Everything's going to be fine. You're skinny now, you have the sexiest outfit ever, and we're seniors now! It's not like we have to be worried about someone stealing our lunch."

I laughed and smoothed some brown eyeshadow onto her eyelid.

"It's not that," I said, trying to focus on her makeup. It was the first day of school. If she didn't care what she looked like, so be it! But I cared, and I wanted my best friend to have the attention of all the guys.

"Then what is it?"

"I gained five pounds over the summer … I just don't want anyone to notice."

She stared at me, open-mouthed. She looked shocked, sad, and angry all at the same time. "Who the fuck would notice that?"

I put the makeup bag away, averting my eyes to the floor. For her, five pounds was no big deal. The kid ate like crap, rarely worked out, and was perpetually skinny. If she gained five pounds, she might actually look better. For the "used-to-be-fat" girl, five pounds is a huge deal. Five pounds could lead to ten, and then twenty, and then I could be back at 185 pounds.

She took my arm and yanked me up to the mirrors. I stared at myself. Clear complexion. Brown eyes. Long hair. Fat arms. Fat legs. And a pocket of blubber on my lower stomach.

"Don't you see how beautiful you are?" she asked.

I just stared at my reflection, counting all the fat parts. I got up to ten.

\*\*\*

"How's my favorite busser doing today?" I walked in through the "help entrance" of Ted's Pub right on time, wearing my ever-so-stylish navy blue Ted's button-down shirt and yoga pants. And just like every time I worked, I walked into the kitchen and there was the cook, Tyler, smiling over at me. He wasn't a musician like me, but he'd listened to my demo before, went to my gigs, and totally supported my music.

I walked away from the kitchen area toward the hostess desk. There were all the waitresses, smiling over at me. I said my hellos and punched in. There were no tables that needed to be set, but I had to take a few bus buckets from the waitress stations to the kitchen, take out the garbage, and fill all the bins with ice. By the time it was done, a half hour of my shift was over and I had nothing else to do. No one had come in, and the ten parties that were in the restaurant were still eating.

I leaned against the wall beside the hostess desk and waited. Waited for customers or for Autumn, the hostess, to let me leave.

"So, guys, what do you think? Is it going to be busy tonight?" Autumn asked.

"No way. It's the first day of school," I said, convincing myself.

"You're creating bad karma for my girls," she said, then smiled. "Maybe if we all think it'll be busy, it will be." We all laughed, and Autumn changed the subject. If it wasn't busy, we made little to no money. But, on the bright side, I wouldn't be running around like a chicken with my head cut off if it was slow. I had no energy to do that.

"Remember, Dan is the manager tonight, so everyone should be on their best behavior. I don't want to have to protect any of my girls today ... especially not my busser." Autumn grinned over at me.

She was referring to last week. I'd left a bit early on my Friday-night shift to go to a party, and I'd forgotten to bring out a keg. Dan had a hissy fit, and from what I heard from all the waitresses, it was not pretty. I was still the best busser on staff, but Dan was not a fan of mistakes. He liked things at the restaurant to run smoothly, and I actually respected him for that.

Anyway, Autumn had stuck up for me, reminding him that she was the one who had let me leave early. She also reminded him that I was the head busser and that I worked the hardest. From what I heard from

Ashley, it really calmed him down, and he forgot all about it.

"Sorry," I said, laughing. "That whole argument was so worth it, though. The party was really fun." I remembered Friday night very well and couldn't stop smiling when I thought about it.

"Oh, god. How many boys did you meet at the party?" one of the girls joked. Everyone at the restaurant knew I had a lot of boyfriends. They knew partly because I brought the boys there for dinner a lot and also because I told the girls everything.

"Just one boy. He's sweet, funny, and athletic. Oh, wait—did I mention he's in college?" I smiled from ear to ear. Let's be honest, I was damn proud of myself. Damien really was a triple threat, and he had hooked up with *me* …

Autumn started asking me questions, and just when I told her that "no, he isn't a virgin," Devan walked over to the computer to punch in.

"Sorry, I don't mean to interrupt." His eyes found mine and held, just like they always did. He always seemed to pop up at the worst times.

"Oh, hey, Devan," I said, walking toward the bar and of course away from him and the awkward conversation. I turned my head back toward the hostess station, and all the waitresses still standing there were laughing.

They all knew we'd hooked up, and we were still very uncomfortable around each other. They knew just how awful it was when Devan worked with me and when he saw me. He flirted with me, he teased me, and he made me fall for him over and over again. I didn't just want to hook up with him anymore; I wanted to be his girlfriend. All these other guys I hung out with and hooked up with had potential, but they weren't Devan. They didn't make me melt like he did.

I had always been talkative and outgoing. My mom said that was because I was always onstage and singing. So guys didn't really make me nervous. Except Devan. Devan made me nervous. He made my whole body tingle. Sexually, I wanted him more than any other guy. Emotionally, I just wanted to peel down those dangerous layers of his. I wanted him to open up to me. I could be good for him if he'd just let me.

I went to the bar in long, quick strides. I needed to get away from Devan. I could catch my breath when I was a few feet away.

"You came over here awful fast," Lucas said from behind me. He was pouring some chocolate concoction into a martini glass. I inhaled through my nose, taking in all of the chocolate smell. Boy, did I love chocolate. Maybe even more than boys.

The smell reminded me just how hungry I was. To

get rid of the five pounds I'd gained over the summer, I was on a very strict diet. I was running every day for an hour, only eating when I absolutely had to, and drinking water constantly.

"You need to get over him, you know," Lucas said and walked away toward the end of the bar. He placed a glass down, chatted for a second with a customer, and came right back to me. I still didn't know how to respond. I wasn't shocked that Lucas knew. *Everyone* knew. Just like high school, the girls at a restaurant know how to spread gossip.

"I am over him. It's been a really long time since that night."

He laughed and shook his head. He pivoted to his right and took a plate from a customer who was done eating. He handed the plate to me, which I put into the bar's bus bucket.

"You're an awful liar. I wish you would just talk to him and stop pretending nothing's wrong. I know you're sad about what happened between you two."

"I am obviously disappointed. I want to be with him." Lucas's eyes cocked to his left, and he nudged his head in that direction. I looked to my left, and there was Devan walking toward me. Every time I saw him, I pictured us together. Him holding me when I was scared, kissing me in the twilight, us going out on

Saturday nights to the movies and to dinner.

Why wasn't he into me? There must have been something seriously wrong with me. It had to be that I was too fat. He was rugged, tall, and thin. He probably wanted someone with a similar body type. Why would any boy as cute as him want a fat girl like me?

"All right, I'll see you later."

"Don't think this conversation's over, young lady!" Lucas joked.

I laughed and started walking toward Devan. Again, I took long strides, hoping that when we passed each other it wouldn't be for longer than a few seconds. The theory, though plausible, didn't pan out because the speed landed me on my ass.

The first pain I felt was in my head. I'd hit my head pretty hard on the tile floor.

"Whoa, are you okay?" Devan knelt on the ground next to me. I opened my eyes, and his face was inches from mine. I could feel his breath on my cheeks.

"I'm ... " I closed my eyes and focused on the pain. My ass was totally going to have a bruise, and so was the elbow that I'd landed on. But, that didn't make me nervous ... the banging in my head was the real problem.

Within a few seconds, everyone was around us, and Devan backed up just a tad. Lucas, Autumn, and the girls huddled around Devan and me.

"Hey, sweetie, what hurts?" I wasn't completely sure who said it, and I honestly didn't care. All I could do was shake my head and blink. I felt like I was in a different world. Everything was in slow motion. I could barely hear the people around me; all I could focus on was the blinding pain in my head.

"She hit her head pretty hard," Devan said and put a hand behind my head, getting close to my face again. "Hey, can you hear us?"

I shook my head and started moving my legs underneath me. I needed to stand—maybe that would help.

Devan took my arm and pulled me up to him. I felt just fine as I stood, but then it all seemed to come crashing down. Within a second, I couldn't breathe, and both of my arms came around Devan's shoulders. My head bowed down, and tears starting falling from my eyes.

"Hey, don't cry, Stacey. Are you okay?" Devan brought my face to his shoulder and held on. His body wrapped around mine and held. Despite Devan's kind words, I couldn't stop sobbing into his polo shirt. And let's be honest, this wasn't the pretty, sweet, nice cry. This was the ugly cry. The cry I preferred to do alone in my room with the door locked.

"My head … " was all I could get out as I hiccupped into his shoulder. I opened my eyes through the searing pain and saw the huge stain on his bright blue polo. Not only was there a spot from my tears, but long streaks of my mascara, too. I swallowed and closed my eyes again. I wasn't sure I could handle this awful pain anymore. It was as though someone was smashing my head with a hammer.

I had never experienced anything like this in my life. I mean, sure, my period was so bad in the beginning that I needed a birth control prescription. But this was totally different. This pain made me feel like I was going to throw up.

"She needs to go to the hospital," Autumn said. I was still holding on to Devan, gripping his shoulders. I didn't know what would happen if I let go.

"I can take her," Devan said all too quickly. "I'll call her mom from her phone on the way there."

"No, I'll take her!" Lucas and Autumn said in unison.

"You two have the most important jobs in here. Let me take her." Everyone seemed to agree, and before I could protest, Devan was picking me up in his strong arms and taking me to his car. The last thing I remembered was looking up into the front seat and seeing Devan, and his ginger hair, driving us away.

# Chapter Two

When I woke up, the first things I noticed were the white walls and a distinct smell of Lysol. As I looked around more and more, I saw all of the monitors and machines surrounding me. I was in a hospital. Frightened, I looked down to find that I was also in a hospital gown, my right arm had an IV inside it, and my left arm was bandaged.

I heard a door open, and before I knew it, Devan was sitting in a chair beside the night table. He handed me a cup of cold water.

"How do you feel?" he asked, moving closer to me.

I took a sip and exhaled. "Fine. My head feels a lot better." I started to set the cup down on the table, but

Devan did it for me.

"Good, I'm glad. Your sister Danielle should be here any minute." He looked at me questioningly, as if I'd told him things. "By the way, I had no idea your dad commuted that far away," he added. My dad was a professor and, being that it was so hard to find jobs in my dad's field at the time, he'd taken a job a few hours away. We really didn't want to move, so we found a way to adapt. We commuted to see each other. My mom and I visited him often in the summer, but when school started, my mom would take the trips on her own and let my older sister Danielle stay with me at home.

"Yeah, she left last night. She just got there today," I said, putting my head back on the pillow. Devan was here … with me. Devan. My nemesis-slash-lover was taking care of me.

"She sounded pretty nervous on the phone when I called her," he said with a laugh. "And it didn't seem like she liked me very much." That made me smile, too. My mom hated him; she hated that he'd made me cry.

"That's because she doesn't." I smiled and put my hand on my upper thigh, searching for my cell. "Where's my phone?" He got up and brought my purse over to me. I searched through the mess that was my purse and finally found my phone.

I dialed my sister, who said she'd be there momentarily. Then, deciding that I'd put it off long enough, I dialed my mother's number. She answered on the first ring.

"Baby!" I could tell by her shaky voice that she had been crying.

"Hey, Mommy," I said.

"HOW DO YOU FEEL?" She was screaming into the phone.

"I'm okay, Mom." I knew right about now my mother was pacing back and forth, probably shaking in her size-twelve jeans. I really didn't want her to worry.

"Tell me what happened."

I looked over at Devan, who was staring right at me. He smiled and looked down at the magazine he had on his lap.

"Well, one minute I was walking, and the next the wind was knocked out of me and I was on the ground … It just felt really weird. I hit my head, and then Devan picked me up and took me to the emergency room. I guess I passed out in the car because I woke up in a hospital bed."

My mom sobbed into the phone; I could hear her catching her breath. "I can't believe I'm not by your bedside. I'm driving home now."

"Mom, Dad needs you to stay there with him. You haven't seen him in a while. I'm just fine here. Danielle will be here in a second. We can do this together." I really wanted her to come home, but I knew that my dad needed her more than I did. He was almost always alone when he was in a different city. I had Danielle, and we would be fine.

I turned to Devan, who was watching me intently. He seemed enthralled by everything I did, and also very nervous. I wondered if he was scared because of my health, or because my mom knew what he'd done to me.

"Devan's with me now, though, Mom. I don't want to be rude."

"Okay, sweetie. Let me know when you speak to a doctor." That's where the conversation ended.

"She was crying," I said, smiling weakly over at Devan.

"I could hear." He laughed. "I'm not surprised she reacted that way. Aren't you and your mom really close?"

"Beyond close. I literally have her exact personality," I said, smiling. I really did wish my mom were there. I needed her by my side. I tried to blink back the tears that suddenly came to my eyes. Just talking about my mom made me miss her.

"Hey, whoa … " Devan pulled his chair closer to my bed. His concern was all over his face. Devan, the rebel, was suddenly becoming much more sensitive to ensure that I was okay. It made me feel special.

"You really don't need to do this for me, you know. This doesn't make sense. We're still on awkward terms." My issues with Devan were definitely not resolved yet. We barely said anything at work to each other besides "Hey," "Bye," and "Can you carry this for me?" I wasn't completely sure if we were even friends. And yet, I felt the need to explain to him why I was upset.

"My mom and sister aren't here, I don't know if I killed my brain in that fall, and the doctor's taking way too long to come in and tell me," I groaned, and hiccupped, trying to hold back the "ugly cry." I didn't want to cry at all, and crying in front of Devan was even worse. "Ugh, why am I crying?"

He took my hand while I used my free one to wipe tears from my cheeks.

"I know why you're crying. You're scared." He squeezed my hand a little harder, just as Danielle walked through the door. She was wearing her lawyer clothes: a perfectly ironed pair of black slacks and a pink blouse. She looked beautiful, as usual. Her face was flushed, and she was limping just a tad. I laughed and looked down to her heels. That explained the limp. She could never handle heels.

"Nice heels," I said, smiling up at my sister. She walked swiftly toward me, and her arms came around my shoulders. She held on tight.

"Are you okay?" she asked, still holding me. "You scared the shit out of me." She let go, and when she pulled away, I realized she had tears in her eyes.

"I'm okay," I said, looking down to the hand that was still holding on to Devan's. My sister's eyes glared over at Devan … and then she looked back at me. She knew the whole story about what happened with Devan, and she was not his biggest fan.

"Thank you for calling me, Devan, and bringing her here. I've got it from here if you have something else to do." Her words were very professional, but I know that she was mentally beating him senseless. It didn't matter that he'd brought me to the hospital; he was still an asshole in Danielle's book.

"Actually, I do have to get back to work … " he said, moving in closer toward me. His arms came around me, and my whole body tensed. I took breaths of his cologne. I exhaled as he let go and stared into his eyes. He really was the perfect guy. He was sexy as fuck, a great kisser, and, sexually, made me feel frustrated and enticed and scared all at the same time … He made me feel like a woman. But today, he'd shown me that he was sensitive and had a sweet side.

"Devan, how can I ever thank you?" I said, trying to keep my voice from shaking.

"You don't need to. You would have done the same for me." He said his good-byes to Danielle, and before I knew it, he was gone. I looked up to my shocked sister.

"Oh. My. God!" I squealed as Danielle laughed and sat next to me on the bed.

"I still hate him," she said. I hugged her hard. "And his stupid red hair." I laughed. She was not a "ginger-hater" … She just needed a reason to insult him. And apparently it was going to be his hair at that moment.

There was a knock on the door, and a group of doctors came into my room.

"Hello, Stacey. I'm Doctor Channing, and these are my interns." I smiled, shaking my head. This was just like my absolute favorite show, *Grey's Anatomy*! I smiled and wondered who were best friends out of the group of six, who was having sex with each other, and who was most like my very favorite character, Christina. I looked over to Danielle, who was grinning just as big as I was. We were both *Grey's Anatomy* junkies.

"It's so nice to meet you all," Danielle said, taking

over the mom role. Her lawyer voice was on instantly when she spoke to them.

"Well, we should probably get right to it, Stacey ..." The head doctor looked very serious. My body tensed. Was there any way my eating disorders could be a factor in this? I didn't think so. I just fell.

"You suffered a concussion, which explains the fainting, and the severe migraine," he said, and then looked to the intern at his side, a cue for him to start explaining what else was wrong with me.

The attractive African American doctor started talking now. "You fell as a result of dehydration and malnourishment. Your body collapsed because it had no energy. Your body needs fuel to keep moving and functioning. That means you need to eat." My sister looked over at me with wide eyes. I cleared my throat and shook my head quickly. My eating disorder was not going to be explained to my sister, or any of my family members, for that matter. This problem was mine, and I could handle it on my own.

"I didn't eat today," I said quickly and chuckled to myself. "I promise you, I'm an eater. I'm Italian. Today was the first day of school, though, and I always get really nervous so I don't eat breakfast, and I still felt the same way before lunch. I was planning on having a big burger with French fries after my shift tonight at the pub, but I guess I should have eaten before." I switched my gaze to my sister. I could tell by her facial expression that she believed me. I truly had come up with a story that sounded like something I would do. "I'm sorry. I should have been more careful."

My sister smiled and took my hand in hers. "It's okay. You just need to make sure you're drinking water and eating more often during the day—even when you're nervous!" My sister and I both shook our heads and listened to the doctors once again.

"You can go home now if you feel all right. We'll send you home with pain meds that will put you right to sleep. I'm sure you'll be out of school for a few days. You'll be back by next week, though."

I looked at the doctors, shocked. I was missing the beginning of school! I knew that wasn't good, and that my teachers weren't going to have a good first impression of me.

"Okay, that sounds great. Thank you, doctors." My sister shook Dr. Channing's hand, and before we knew it, we were both on the phone with my mother, my other sister, Kara, and my father, letting them know the verdict. By the time we'd told the family what the doctors said, I'd been discharged and we were heading to the car.

When I got home, I went directly to my messy

bedroom. I turned the lights off and pulled the covers over my head. I had a faint headache, and with each passing minute, I could feel it more and more.

"Here, why don't you eat this, drink all this water, and then take this?" My sister gave me about twenty water crackers, handed me a large glass of ice water, and a large pain pill. I ate one as my sister left, then hid the rest of the crackers under my bed. They had way too many calories. I drank the full glass of water and then took my painkiller. Before I knew it, I was fast asleep.

# Chapter Three

"It's so nice to have you back!" Clare said, hugging me. I held on and smiled. She wasn't the type to show her feelings and tell me she missed me. But, being that Clare was drunk, everything seemed to come out. For that specific reason, I loved when she drank. It was always very fun to watch my oh-so-strong best friend turn into a softy like me.

"I know. I missed partying."

We were at "Old Stony," the universal bonfire spot in the woods on Stone Drive. Old Stony was always fun and a bit rowdy. The reason so many people went to Old Stony was because the cops never came since it was in the middle of the woods. Plus, you had to go off-roading to get there. The path to the bonfire spot was very rocky, and you needed a pickup truck to get up the long hill.

"I missed my wingman!" I laughed and hugged her again. I really did love my best friend.

Surrounding us was a group of about thirty teens. There were kegs in three of the guys' trucks, and weed was being passed around continuously. Since our friend Ryan was driving us home, we were both heading down the wasted path. She was much more trashed than I was, though. I figured since I had taken a painkiller in the morning for my headache, getting shit-faced wasn't the best idea. I decided to get high instead.

"Do you want some?" A tall, dark, and handsome guy came up from behind me and wrapped his right arm around my waist. He used his other arm to hold a joint out to me. I leaned into him, taking his whole body in. He was definitely toned and muscular. He made me feel small, just like Devan. I couldn't say no to a hottie like him.

I took the joint from his hand and held it to my lips. I inhaled for a few seconds, feeling the heat in the back of my throat before releasing the smoke. *Mmm.* It felt so good. I handed Clare the joint, and she walked over to our other friends.

"So what's your name, cutie?" Both hands came around me, and he was pushing me closer to his body.

"Stacey." I breathed, pushing my head back onto his left shoulder, exposing one side of my neck. His lips came down on my neck and kissed me hard. I shifted my body to one side and turned to face him. This boy was much cuter than I had thought. He had a beautiful, tan face and a strong body.

His hands came to the small of my back, grazing the line where my tank top and shorts did not meet. He was in search of skin.

"I'm … " He pulled my waist toward him, and I went onto my tiptoes just before I kissed him. My lips held on to his, and I nibbled on his bottom lip. This made his whole body tense, and I really liked that. I liked making him feel good. "I'm Mike. Mike Atone."

We both laughed and continued kissing, exploring each other. We both knew that we didn't give a shit what each other's names were. He was here for one reason and one reason only.

All I wanted was more as his hands came down to my cleavage.

"Do you have a car?" I asked, looking up into his dark eyes. Without words, he led me in the direction of the parking area.

"Baby, you're so fucking sexy. That ass … "

His voice trailed off as we got into his truck. Within seconds, his body was on top of mine. The weed was finally starting to hit me now; my brain felt cloudy. I felt like I couldn't control what my body did.

My hands felt his stomach, and just as I'd suspected, he had a perfectly sculpted six-pack. Mike definitely spent his time in the gym. I worked my hands up and pulled the T-shirt over his head. I looked over his body and saw his checkered boxers. I wanted them off. I slowly glided off his jeans, which was sort of a challenge in the back seat.

I switched positions now, getting on top. I started taking the control and gliding off his boxers. He was so hard, and I couldn't believe that was from me. I'd say he was about seven or eight inches with a slight crook to the right side. He was big. *Really* big. And I wondered how I was going to fit him inside my mouth.

I straddled his torso and leaned my butt on his lap. This way, he could see the full view. My hands came to the bottom of my tank top, and I lifted it off with ease. My red bra was perfect for the occasion. A smile curled over his lips, and he sighed as I put my hands behind my back and slowly unhooked my bra.

My breasts spilled out as I took them out of the cups. His hands instantly reached to them, filling his hands with my boobs.

"Oh, baby … you're so soft." His fingertips circled my nipples, first slowly and gently … but then he started squeezing. My nipples were hard now and elongated from his touch. I threw my head back and moaned as he lifted his body up and brought his lips to my nipple.

He licked around my right breast first, clenching onto my left one. His tongue came around my nipple, and then he started biting me. I was so wet now. All I could focus on was his touch … I needed more from him. I wanted more.

"I think we should take your pants off, babe, see if you're ready for me." My mouth dropped open just a tad as I realized what he was saying. He wanted to have sex tonight. He didn't just want a blowjob. He wanted to be inside me … He wanted to take my virginity.

I let him take my shorts off, and my black boy-short panties. The anticipation was killing me now. *What was it going to feel like? Was I going to orgasm? Was it going to hurt?* My mind raced as his hands came down to the opening of my vagina. He started off slow, using one finger horizontally … brushing back and forth, back and forth. I groaned, savoring his touch.

After a few seconds, though, it became hard. He stopped with the slow, gentle touch, and he was ramming fingers inside of me. My body jumped as he put three inside me. This didn't feel good. It just hurt. My body and vagina tensed as he kept sticking one more finger inside me.

"Ow," I said, looking down at him. "That doesn't feel good, you know."

His hands left my sex, and he brought his fingers toward my mouth. He didn't ask, didn't question … he just stuck his fingers in my mouth, insinuating that I should lick them. I licked away the salty-tasting substance quickly and moved my head away from his hands. I wanted to get as far away from this boy as possible. This wasn't sexy anymore; it was uncomfortable and weird.

"Baby, I want you on the bottom. I want to look at your eyes cloud while I stick my dick inside of your wet pussy. Baby, you're so tight; I want you to wrap right around me." I stared at him, shocked, trying to make my decision. Was I really doing this? Getting rid of my virginity with someone who couldn't make me feel good when he fingered me? I wasn't sure if it was a good idea.

Before I could make a decision, he was picking me up and positioning me below him. It was all so fast.

"Oh, baby, you're still so wet for me." I almost laughed at that. I wasn't wet at all anymore.

It all seemed to happen at once. One minute, Mike

was teasing me. The next, he was going inside me … hard. He got about halfway in when I screamed. *Oh. My. God.* The pain took my breath away.

"Whoa … Get the fuck off me! Get out!" I screamed. "Get the fuck out of me!" I pushed his body off mine, but he kept struggling to get in.

"Come on, babe," he said. "It'll get better." His hips were moving now, thrusting forward and trying to go farther inside me. I clenched and tears started to spring to my eyes. I didn't want to do this. I really didn't want to do this. This was nothing like I thought it would be.

"No it won't!" I started pushing his shoulders now and hitting his body. It was obvious my blows to his frame weren't affecting him. He was way too strong for me. The tears were really coming down my cheeks now, as his body pounded into mine. He was all the way in. I was completely full.

"Calm down, bitch." His hands held my arms down, keeping me from hitting him.

He started moving really fast. There was no way that this was making love. This was straight fucking. Hard. Fast. Strong. He kept moving, pounding into me. With every thrust, I was in more pain.

"Please! Stop," I started pleading now. I wondered if that would work. He was taking everything from me.

After all those years of no one wanting me, the only person who wanted to take my virginity was a rapist?

I cried, praying for him to finish. I closed my eyes and tried to envision myself somewhere else, somewhere I was happy. I thought of my family, all piled in the family room on Christmas morning. I thought of singing. I thought of Clare and me baking cookies and watching movies together. But after just a few seconds of pretending, Mike would hit me, or thrust deeper, and I would be back in reality. I was being raped. I was all alone. I was the damsel in distress. And there was no one there to save me.

\*\*\*

"Are you okay?" was all I could hear after I got out of the car with Mike. I closed the door quickly, and within seconds he was pulling away, leaving me before I told anyone. Everyone surrounded me as I walked toward the bonfire. But I didn't want the attention. I headed back the other way, toward Ryan's truck, and got in the front seat. I sat in the car, hoping to make sense of what had just happened to me.

Ryan, unlike the majority of the people at Old

Stony, was completely sober. He saw me in his truck, and he walked over. He opened his car door and stared at me. I must have looked like a complete mess.

"What happened?" he asked, wrapping his arms around me. Ryan was such a sweet guy. He had dated Clare for a while freshman year, and during that time we had become pretty close. I trusted him, but not enough to tell him that my virginity had been forcibly taken from me.

"I really need to go home," I whispered. When he barely responded, I became more forceful. "Now, Ryan. Where's Clare?" He pointed out Clare behind me, sleeping in the back of the truck. Ryan had Clare and me home within twenty minutes. The whole way home, I wondered, was this my fault? Was I to blame for what had happened to me?

By the time we were home, Clare was still sound asleep. I opened the garage door, and Ryan took her in his arms, bringing her into the house. He set her down on my sofa. I put a blanket on her and kissed her cheek. I really did love her, but I wished she was awake to talk to me.

"Stacey, are you sure you're okay?"

I disregarded the question, being that I was nothing close to okay, and hugged him. "I'll be fine, Ryan. Thank you," I said.

He headed out, and I was all alone again. The house was so quiet, and surprisingly, so was I. I had cried all my tears. I felt so empty, so barren.

"I can't believe this," I whispered under my breath as I walked up the stairs toward the bathroom. I needed a shower more than anything else. I stopped in Danielle's room and told her I was home and that Clare was staying over. When my sister just stirred, heading back to sleep, I stayed in her room for a few minutes, praying that she'd wake up so I could tell her. But she never did, so I headed to the bathroom as planned. I turned the water on warm and then went to the linen closet to get a sponge and a clean towel.

Within minutes, the water was just the right temperature, and I stepped in. I let the water pour down me, hitting my scalp, my shoulders, running down my arms and legs. All I wanted to do was scrub his sweat off my body, scrub all of his semen from my vagina, and scrub away any sign of him touching me, hurting me, being inside me.

I washed and conditioned my hair, and then squeezed a large amount of shower gel onto the sponge. I started with my shoulders, working the sponge down my body slowly. I massaged my breasts and stared down at my arms. There were small bruises on my forearms, and they felt sore, too, as I rubbed the sponge over them. I then went to my legs and my feet ... scrubbing every inch of my body.

When I got out of the shower, I threw all my clothes into my hamper and put on a new pair of panties and my nightgown. As I towel-dried my hair, my phone vibrated.

Devan: Hey, feeling ok?

I scowled down at my phone, shaking my head. Ever since he'd taken me to the hospital, he'd been treating me like we were best friends. When the truth was, we were not. We were coworkers. We'd hooked up. He hurt me. Just because he'd helped me didn't mean he wasn't an asshole.

Stacey: FUCK YOU. Don't treat me like we're friends. You hurt me. I'm not going to pretend like we never hooked up, and you never made me cry. I still hate you. And BTW, I'm not a virgin anymore. I know that's all you care about. Figured you should know. The guy I lost it to is actually a bigger asshole than you. Surprise, surprise.

I smiled at that text and walked downstairs. I totally just won that battle. I sat down on the couch across from sleeping Clare and plugged my phone into its charger. Just as I did that, my phone went off.

Devan: I'm sorry I hurt you. And what happened?

Stacey: I said no. He kept going. I'm sore. That's what fucking happened.

I sent the message, and within a minute, he was calling me. I ignored the call and turned my phone off. Just like every guy, he was an asshole and didn't give a shit about anything besides sex. I wasn't going to talk to a prick like that again. Not even if I still had secret feelings for him.

# Chapter Four

I was sitting in the back of the class on Monday, finally back in school. I was off the pain meds and was feeling just fine. Mentally, things weren't going well, though. I had only told one person what had happened that night. I hadn't even told Clare. I was waiting for the right time, which never seemed to come.

I'd always thought that when I had sex I'd have this great story to tell. A story involving a gorgeous boy who made me feel beautiful, who treated me with respect and love. A guy who got me off and made me feel so good. I still couldn't believe that the guy who was my first did none of that for me.

"Welcome back, Ms. Lorenzo," my English teacher

said to me with a smile. I handed her my makeup work as she walked by me. "How are you feeling? Your mother emailed me about your hospital visit."

"I feel much better. Thank you, Ms. Mallino."

She continued with class, collecting all of the homework and then teaching a lesson on *Romeo & Juliet*. I knew it backward and forward, so I decided to zone out for the day and focus on the cute guy in the corner of the room.

His name was Andrew Champagne, and he was new. On the first day of school, he wore a pair of dark jeans and an Asking Alexandria T-shirt. Today he wore light jeans and a Three Days Grace tee. The kid had good taste in music, which was always a plus for me. He had dark, black hair and smoky eyes. This also was a plus for me. He gave off this vibe ... It was like he didn't really give a fuck. He was a very go-with-the-flow kind of guy. He was also blatantly flirty.

"Ms. Lorenzo?" I looked up to Ms. Mallino. She caught me ... I was totally clocked out. I had no idea what had happened during the whole class. "Seeing that you haven't paid attention for the last hour or so but have been able to stare at Andrew all class, I think you should stand up and read with him." My mouth dropped open, and I instantly blushed. I stood slowly, as did a smiling Andrew from across the room. His eyes locked onto mine. He was totally smirking at me.

"O … okay," I said, slowly standing up. Ms. Mallino handed me a script with a joking smile. She was totally doing this for her enjoyment. She was playing matchmaker.

"What scene?" Andrew asked, looking at the paper.

I smiled, looking up at him. She was having us perform the most romantic scene in the whole piece. "It's the balcony scene," I said. We stood opposite each other at the front of the classroom. Everyone was smiling at us, laughing almost, especially my two friends sitting at the front of the room.

"Start here," Ms. Mallino said, pointing to both of our scripts. "And make it good. Say it like you mean it. If you don't do this well, I'm taking points off your participation grade, Ms. Lorenzo." She winked at both of us and sat down at her desk in the corner of the room, resting her feet on the top of the desk. She was totally into this.

Andrew cleared his throat and took one step closer to me. "O, wilt thou leave me so unsatisfied?"

Andrew's voice was so powerful, deep and strong. He had a man's voice, and Lord, he had a man's body. He was so attractive, about six-foot-one, with a muscular build. Beyond his physical appearance, he seemed really cool and playful. He was totally, without a doubt, flirting with me. He was trying to impress me with his acting too.

"What satisfaction canst thou have to-night?"

He couldn't know that Clare had given me pointers on acting. I knew how to act … and I knew how to play a flirtatious teen girl. I was one! I knew how to make boys want me. Andrew stepped forward now and reached down for my hand. I stared at him, shocked. I was totally holding my breath as his hand held mine. It was so rough and callused. I wanted to feel the rest of his body. Would it be as masculine as his hand?

"The exchange of thy love's faithful vow for mine." He was looking into my eyes now, still holding that slow, playful smile on his lips.

"I gave thee mine before thou didst request it, and yet I would it were to give again."

"Wouldst thou withdraw it? For what purpose, love?" my Romeo said.

"But to be frank, and give it thee again. And yet I wish but for the thing I have: My bounty is as boundless as the sea, my love as deep; the more I give to thee, the more I have, for both are infinite."

With my last words, Andrew took just one more step closer. One minute his hand was holding mine, and then his lips were touching mine. The kiss was soft, delicate. It lingered, and I responded instantly by kissing him back. My body pressed against his, and I sighed as my lips parted and the kiss became more intense. Everything melted around me, and my mind seemed to cloud. I was confused about where I was, and all I could think about was Andrew ... and his sweet lips.

Ms. Mallino started clapping behind us, and I paused, trying to find reality. I realized what had happened, and a well of emotions flooded me, and I was shocked, embarrassed, and also completely turned on all at the same time. I backed away from Andrew first, but his arms were still around me. His eyes opened, and he just stared at me. There was passion in his eyes.

"That was amazing!" Our teacher exclaimed. I looked out at the faces in the class, and they screamed one of two things: shock or joy.

"Damn," Austin, a football player in the front row, said out loud. And with that one word, the whole class started buzzing, some smiling, some clapping, and others shaking their heads with confusion. They saw quite a show, and everyone knew we weren't exactly acting.

The bell rang, and everyone got up quickly, as usual. The other kids and Ms. Mallino filed out of the room, and I stood there, feet planted, not moving an inch. I didn't want to move. Not yet.

"You are a really good kisser," Andrew said very calmly as if he made out with girls in front of his English class at his old school all the time. He let go of my waist and took a step back. Before I could respond, he was walking away toward his desk. I stood there, in the same position I was when he kissed me. I was still taking it all in. He gathered his books off his desk, slipped his cell into his pocket, and headed for the door. He looked back at me for a split second, though, and winked.

That's all it took. One wink … and I was hooked.

***

When I got home, I started with my algebra homework and finished with my AP psychology work. I was already all caught up with my work from when I was sick and finished with my up-to-date work. I was right on schedule, and I felt pretty great about all my classes.

Except English, of course. I didn't know how I was going to even set foot in that class, let alone function in it. How could I? He had kissed me passionately after reciting lines from one of my favorite plays. Even now, after what had happened with Mike, Andrew made me feel like love was still possible. Like I could have the fairy tale I had always dreamed of.

By the time four o'clock rolled around, my doorbell was ringing, and all of my bandmates were at the house. Derek, the guitarist, got there first. He headed in with his blue Fender and large amp. Eli, my drummer, and Jeremy, my bassist, arrived shortly after. Since my dad played drums occasionally, we already had a drum set for Eli set up.

On the way home from school, I had driven to Stop and Shop and used the credit card my mom gave me to buy a large bag of Doritos, Cape Cod Potato Chips, and a few bottles of soda. The boys knew how to eat. They also knew how to make me feel loved and talented. My band made me so happy.

"So, did everyone learn *1985* by Bowling for Soup?" Eli asked from behind the drum set.

"Yes!" we all said in unison. We had a list of songs we had to learn for every practice. This kept us on task and ready for the gigs we had.

Within minutes, we were jamming out to the music. We sounded totally in sync like we'd been playing Bowling for Soup for years.

"Guys, we sound great!" I said, smiling at everyone.

After a few songs, we all sat down on the couch and started eating the junk food I'd bought. We may have only done a few songs, but it was always tiring.

"Guess what I brought!" Jeremy went over to his backpack and stared back at us with a big smile. That crazy, shaggy hair of his fell over his eyes. He was an absolute stoner, but he was adorable. If he hadn't been my bassist, I would have been attracted to him.

"Weed?" Eli asked, walking over to Jeremy's backpack and taking a whiff. Eli's smile told us that Jeremy definitely had something special for us.

"When is Danielle coming home?" Derek asked, walking over to the guys. Derek was the best roller out of the four of us. Jeremy smoked a lot, but nowhere near the amount Derek did.

"She'll be home later on. She has a date," I said, smiling. I knew we were totally taking a weed break, and I couldn't wait to get high with the boys.

The guys and I were on our second bowl pack when I started looking for more food and saying the stupidest shit ever. "I am in love with food," I said, taking a Dorito into my mouth ever so slowly. I was savoring every last morsel of that delicious chip.

"Me too!" Derek said, grabbing a drink. "But cotton mouth makes me want soda too," he said with a laugh. "And a shitload of hot girls!" All of the guys laughed and pointed to me as they always did. We always joked around about having a foursome.

"Or *one* hot girl," Derek said, slapping me on the ass. Now, for Derek, this was normal. Out of the band, he was the most flirtatious. Everyone knew I hooked up with a lot of guys, but Derek … well, he must have had a hundred girls under his belt over the past year. That probably was a result of his killer smile and award-winning personality. Plus, he wasn't just an amazing guitarist; he was the quarterback of our high school's football team. You could tell Derek was a jock from a mile away. He was trim and fit, with a strong, hard jawline. He could be a model if he really wanted to be. He was definitely the most attractive out of the boys.

Jeremy was the definition of a rocker. He had the rock swag. Greasy, long black hair. Every time you saw him he was dressed in jeans two sizes too small and a band T-shirt. Occasionally, he wore eyeliner. When he played, he rarely made mistakes, and everything he played was very edgy. He had a style about him, a spunk. He was sexy, in an obvious way.

Eli was more of a loner. He drew and wrote poems. He was the romantic of the group. He was a sweet, kind guy who was definitely misunderstood. Unlike the other guys, I was pretty sure he was a virgin. Eli had these kind eyes, and when he stared at you, somehow everything seemed to feel okay. His beautiful, baby-blue eyes were hard to turn away from. He had softer features than the other boys and a younger-looking face. His hair was in-between Derek and Jeremy's, not super long but not buzzed. His brown hair, gorgeous eyes, and smile were definitely very attractive, but his personality was what I loved. He was always willing to lend a helping hand and an attentive ear.

"Speaking of our hot girl, I heard the new kid kissed you in Mallino's class today," Derek said, hugging me from behind and pushing his limits by grazing his hands up against my hips. I slapped him playfully, and he backed off.

I laughed at his stupidity and stumbled before sitting back on the couch. "Guys, I feel pretty fucked up." My eyes felt shady, I had a faint headache, and the back of my throat burned from all the smoke. "Everything just feels weird."

Eli pushed his glass of soda toward me. "Drink that; it'll help." I smiled at Eli, wrapping my arm around his. He was always a sweetheart. He always made sure I was okay.

"Don't change the subject!" Jeremy said, smiling and putting a chip in his mouth. "I heard you moaned and basically begged him to go inside that tight pussy of yours."

"Excuse me!" I said.

"Oh, come on." Eli put his hand on my leg, quickly

getting my attention. "Guys talk about you, Stacey." Now I was really shocked. Even Eli believed these guys?

"I heard you give an awesome blowjob, too," Derek said, lying back on the floor. He was definitely fucked up because he was looking up at the ceiling like it was the coolest thing he'd ever seen in his life. "And I've made it my mission to get you drunk enough that you give us all one in the same night. That way we can torture you for the rest of your life."

I slapped him harder now. I started laughing so hard I was crying, snorting and hitting my knee just as the boys were. But then another switch seemed to turn on because the laughter became tears. My head was in my hands as I sobbed in front of the guys.

"Stace?" Eli said, and started hugging me. "What's wrong?" Even when Eli was high, he was still focused on the well-being of others, especially me.

"I'm fine," I whimpered. The boys gathered around me, wide-eyed. Derek and Jeremy pretended not to be sensitive, but I could tell they'd softened when they saw the tears fill my eyes. "I just had a bad weekend."

"Tell us what's wrong," Jeremy said, frowning.

I wiped the tears away from my eyes and took a deep breath. Hiccups and sobs escaped my mouth. "I can't tell you." If I told them what had happened with

Mike, it wouldn't change anything. I would still not be a virgin anymore. I would still be a rape victim. I would still hate what Mike had done to me.

"Yes, you can," they all spoke in unison again. I shook my head but realized they were right. I could tell them anything.

"I'm not a virgin anymore," I said. "I was at a party, and this guy smoked with me, and then we started hooking up in his truck. It was good in the beginning and then got really aggressive. I told him to stop, but he kept going. I hit him, and he still didn't stop." I lifted my sleeve to show them the bruises from his hard hands holding me down. Eli's and Jeremy's faces reddened with anger, but not like Derek's did. His face looked like a tomato, and he was instantly on his feet.

"I'll fucking kill that son of a bitch."

"We all will!" Jeremy said, and stood with Derek. They both were pacing now, just like boys did when they didn't know how to help. But Eli, the sensitive one, took me in his arms, brushing his fingers through my hair.

"His name's Mike Atone." I gave his name out freely, hoping to God that he ended up with a black eye and a missing dick.

# Chapter Five

After band practice ended and the boys had all left, I wrote a quick note to my sister and headed to pick up Clare. We had a dinner date, and I really needed to see her. She still didn't know about Mike, and she didn't know what had been eating away at me for the past few days. I also had to tell her about Andrew. I needed her advice more than ever.

"Hey!" I said, unlocking my car doors. She got in, dressed in her usual jeans and T-shirt. No makeup, of course.

"You seem happy," she said, pointing to my eyes. I looked in the mirror and saw just how red they were. I definitely wasn't high anymore, because I didn't feel shady at all. It must have been from the crying.

"I smoked with the guys," I said, smirking. "Sorry." She shrugged. She knew she wasn't one to talk; she smoked regularly with her brothers and her other friends.

"So, where to?" she asked, buckling her seatbelt. Clare had had a run-in with a deer last summer, and when the deer won, she ended up having a lot of back issues from it. Ever since, she'd been the seatbelt police.

"We could go to the pub," I said, craving my favorite chopped salad.

"What do you eat there?" she asked, frowning just a bit. I knew where she wanted to go. She wanted to go to Leo's Pizzeria, where she could eat carbohydrates, carbohydrates, and more carbohydrates. I shook my head.

"You can get salads there," I said, smiling. "Not like that matters to you. They have awesome fries, burgers, sandwiches. The pasta primavera is insane … " I looked at her with pleading eyes. "How about this … If you go eat there with me, I'll take you to Stop and Shop after to get candy. My treat." She agreed finally, and we headed to the pub.

Once inside, we were seated in the back room. I chatted with a few of the waitresses, and then one of the girls came over to take our order.

"Hey, you. How are you feeling?" She gave me a quick hug and said hello to Clare. Everyone knew she was my best friend.

"Much better. I'm not taking any more pain medication, and the headaches are completely gone. I'm just tired sometimes, but they said that's normal. I feel much better."

"What was that like? Watching her hit her head like that?" Clare asked our waitress. "I would have had a heart attack." She shook her head and smiled.

"Everyone was pretty calm. Devan looked the most shaken up. When he came back to work the last two hours or so of his shift, the kid dropped, like, twelve glasses. That's a record."

I stared at our waitress, shocked. I had dropped many glasses during my career at the pub, but I had never dropped that many in one night. He must have been really nervous about me.

There it was again, the instant pain in my stomach. My relationship with Devan made me physically sick. Sometimes, he made me feel like he really cared about me. But other times, he made me feel like I was worthless like he didn't care about me at all.

"Wow," I said, and then was speechless.

"Wow's right," Clare said with a smile. She wasn't

Devan's biggest fan, but she knew I still had feelings for him. She really just wanted me to be happy.

"Here he is now," our waitress said, waving Devan over. Apparently he was picking up a shift.

He smiled over at me and waved. "I'll be over in a second!" he called.

My face flushed, and I stared down at the menu in my hands. *Oh. My. God. Oh. My. God.* This was the first time I'd seen him since I'd texted him about Mike. *What was he going to say? Was he going to bring it up?* I wanted to go die in a hole.

"Oh, shit." Clare laughed. Everyone really did get off on my embarrassment.

"What were you thinking for drinks and dinner?" Our waitress asked us.

"Diet Coke and a chopped salad, dressing on the side," I said.

"Can I have a regular Coke and a medium-rare burger with French fries? Thanks." There Clare went, going hard as always. And she couldn't be skinnier.

"I hate you. You're supposed to be fatter." She laughed and shrugged, giving over her menu. Just as we were all set, Devan was heading in our direction with a big smile on his face. He seemed surprisingly fine, even though I'd sent him angry messages and then ignored all of his calls.

"Hey," he said to both of us. I introduced him to Clare, and he was very polite and sweet. "How do you feel?"

"I feel great. I haven't had any symptoms since Saturday," I said, smiling up at that gorgeous face of his.

Why couldn't he just use this time to ask me out? It would be such a simple conversation. *I'm sorry I hurt you. I love you. Date me.*

"That's great," he said, genuinely smiling. He really did care how I was feeling. I could tell because the smile met his eyes.

"You know, when I heard the story about you picking up my best friend and carrying her to your car and taking her to the hospital … I thought it was a fairy tale," Clare said. She kept looking back and forth between the two of us. She obviously noticed our chemistry. It was almost like Clare was trying to help me with Devan. I didn't know if that was such a good idea. He still treated me poorly occasionally, and he wouldn't tell me how he was feeling. We were still in limbo.

He laughed and changed the subject. "Hey, Clare, is it okay if I take Stacey in the back with me for a minute? Dan said he wanted to speak with her, and now he won't have to call her." Clare smirked and shook her head. He was obviously lying. *He* wanted to talk to me.

He led me back to the kitchen and over by the dishwashers. When he turned around and stared at me, his expression completely changed. His face was cold, hard. He was angry.

"What?" I asked, confused by the mood change.

"You can't tell me something like that and then ignore my phone calls. I was petrified. You never told me what happened." He was really raising his voice now, and I was starting to get scared.

"Please don't yell at me," I said, taking a step back from him. Mike had restrained me that night, used all of his strength to take control of me. I wasn't going to let Devan do that now.

I was shaking, staring at his angry face. I was defenseless again. In the back of the kitchen, where no one could see me. He could hurt me just like Mike had.

"Hey, whoa … " Devan stepped toward me, and his arms came around me. "What's wrong?"

"Don't hit me." It was the only response I could come up with. His face morphed, and I saw about a hundred different emotions written all over it, including anger, confusion, and sadness.

"I would never hit you." He held on a little tighter now. I wanted his arms around me forever. He was right. He wouldn't hit me, even when he was angry. He was the one holding me when I was scared, not the one making me feel scared.

His hands brushed my hair at the back of my neck. This made my whole body tingle. Just one, romantic gesture, and my whole body was going into seizure mode. He made my body experience things I couldn't with any other guy.

"Why are you so scared? What happened?" He let my hair go and moved just a tad away from me. His arms were still around my waist, but now we were facing each other, looking into each other's eyes.

"I told you what happened."

Devan was shaking his head now. "He raped you, didn't he?" Devan whispered. He said it softly as if it was a word that scared the shit out of him. It was a hard word, a mean word, a word that should almost be whispered instead of spoken. I closed my eyes and tried to find my happy place. I wasn't going to start crying; I couldn't stop once I started.

"Who is this guy?" His words were soft, calming.

"I can't tell you," I said, starting to walk back to my table and to Clare.

"Why can't you?"

I suddenly realized that Devan wasn't going to make anything better. Like always, he would be great for a few days and then disappear. I didn't want to confide in him. How could I trust him when he was so inconsistent?

"Because you're not my boyfriend! What are we even doing? Stop playing mind games with me and pretending like you care! If you really cared, I'd be yours."

He called after me, but I just kept walking away from his stupidity and ignorance.

\*\*\*

"I need to tell you something," I said to Clare, who was just getting out of the car to go into her house. I couldn't put it off anymore.

"What's up?" she asked, smiling. She looked so happy right at that moment. She had no idea what she was about to hear.

"You remember how we went to Old Stony on Saturday?"

"And I got so drunk Ryan carried me to your couch? No, I don't really remember much of it at all," she admitted.

"I need to talk to you about that night."

"What about it?" she asked, closing the passenger door and leaning through the open window.

"Well, I was with this guy Mike … " I was crying now. I didn't know how to tell my best friend that not only was I not a virgin and the boy had raped me but that I hadn't told her for two days.

She opened the passenger door again and sat back down. She took my hand and waited for me to finish.

"We were just hooking up. And he fingered me. It was good in the beginning, and then it got violent. And then he wanted to have sex, and I wanted to, but I wasn't completely sure what I wanted to do. I was so fucked up, I couldn't think straight," I said, rambling. She just kept shaking her head, her eyes locked on mine. She was so worried. "And then he went inside, and I screamed, and it was really bad and awful and I told him to stop. He kept going."

Her face instantly turned from shocked to horrified. "He did *what*?" Just like my bandmates, I knew that all she wanted to do was beat Mike's face in. Like I said, she was a boy at heart. I disregarded her anger and kept going, rushing through the story, trying to just pull off the Band-Aid as quickly as possible. Clare wiped a few tears from my cheeks.

"I hit him, but it didn't matter. He was so strong." I took a deep breath and hoped to God she wouldn't hate me for what I was about to say. We had a really honest friendship; we told each other everything. I didn't want her to think I didn't trust her. "I was gonna tell you that night, but you were drunk and passed out. I'm sorry I didn't tell you sooner. I didn't know how to tell you."

Her arms came around me, and she held on. Neither of us said a word for a good ten minutes, just held each other and rocked back and forth. I knew she was on my side. That was all I needed.

# Chapter Six

By the time Friday rolled around, I was in an awful mood. For some reason, it felt like everything good that happened wasn't working out, and everything that sucked was becoming much worse.

For starters, Andrew had barely even looked at me in class. I wasn't sure if he was embarrassed or just not interested. The kid was completely and utterly obtuse. Every day I'd walk into class in my best clothes, and with my hair and makeup absolutely perfect, and for some reason it seemed like he didn't even notice. The class was boring as hell too ... Every class I was in was boring. I couldn't focus in chemistry or algebra because both of my teachers had the most monotone voices ever. And my best classes (history and English) were way too easy. Last but not least, AP Psychology was starting to take over all of my free time. There was constant homework, assignments, and tests, and it was starting to give me anxiety (ironically).

The next issue was that Devan hadn't even bothered to call me. I'd texted him repeatedly, trying to sort things out … and I never got a response. The thought of him hating me made me want to cry. I totally cared about him, and I wasn't even sure why. There was something about him that I just could not get out of my head.

Another thing I hated was the fact that my mom wasn't home. I really missed her. Danielle and I were getting along just fine—cooking, cleaning, working. We had our lives without Mom down to a science … but it was so much better when she was home. Plus, I hadn't seen my other sister, Kara, or her fiancé, Fred, in months. They were going down to visit my dad with my mom this weekend. I wished I were going too. I wanted to see Mom, Dad, Kara, and Fred. I wanted to get away from Rhode Island.

The worst problem of all was Mike. As every day passed, I felt more and more alone because of what he did to me. The only people who knew were Devan, Clare, and my band members. Devan wasn't speaking to me, my band had been giving me space (because they knew I wasn't up to discussing it), and Clare was almost *too* supportive. She always wanted to talk about what happened, to make me feel better … when really I just needed to get my mind *off* of it.

When school was over that day, I drove home and put on my sneakers. Since I'd eaten breakfast (Greek yogurt) and a snack (banana), I figured it was definitely time to burn some calories. I started off slow, walking around my neighborhood until my body was pumped and ready for action.

After the five-minute walk, though, I was flying. Pushing, pumping, pounding across the pavement. I ran hard and fast, totally focused. I wasn't allowed to stop today, despite the high temperature and blazing humidity. This was the only way to take five pounds off. I had to work at it.

"Stacey?" In front of me stood Frank, my neighbor, taking the mail out of his family's mailbox. I smiled and waved, hoping he would notice I wanted to keep running and not make me stop. He started walking toward me, though, so I slowed down.

"Hey, Frank," I panted, turning my iPod off so I could hear him. "What's up?"

He looked all too happy to see me, but his face looked confused. "You look … "

I laughed, understanding his confusion now. He had been away at college so he hadn't seen me since I lost all of the weight. *Everyone* had this reaction.

"Fantastic," he finished.

He didn't look too bad himself. Frank had dark features, and he had an average body type. He was definitely attractive, but he had some meat on his bones. He was tall, tan, and beyond handsome. He had a sweet face and a crooked smile that I loved. But I'd never thought of him intimately. He was just a friend.

"Thanks, Frank. Exercise is key." I smiled now, looking up into his eyes. The sun was shining, and man it made him look even better. The sun reflected off his blue eyes … it was absolutely stunning.

"So, how's everything been, Stace? Miss me around school?" I actually did. Frank had shown me around Ridgefield on my first day of school freshman year, always introduced me to his cute friends (even when I was fat), and drove his sister and me to school all year junior year. He never even let me pay him for gas.

"Of course I do. What about you? How's college?" He was a sophomore.

"It's great, Stacey. But I miss home. That's why I'm here; chilling with the guys tonight and the family tomorrow."

"Well, that sounds like just what you need." I really did miss Frank, but all I needed to do right then was burn calories. It was all I could think of. I had eaten a lot today, and I needed to burn it off. Frank was preventing that.

"So … " I started to end the conversation, hoping to start my run again before I stopped sweating. But then Frank cut me off.

"What are you doing tomorrow night, Stacey?"

My jaw dropped. *What the hell? Frank? Neighbor and friend? Asking me out? On a date?*

"Probably going to a party, why?"

He smirked now, but I could tell by his expression that he was just a bit nervous. "I miss you, Stace. And I think it's time we actually do something about this chemistry between us." Now I was really shocked. I mean, I definitely thought Frank was hot, that was for sure. But I didn't think he felt the same way. "What if I pick you up at eight o'clock, and I'll bring you to a party?"

"That actually sounds really amazing, Frank. I'll see you then." I hugged him quickly, hoping he couldn't feel the sweat through my shirt, and headed in the opposite direction. The rest of the run home, I was smiling. Frank wanted to date me.

The whole run, I stayed focused. Every time I

wanted to slow my stride and start walking, I thought of Frank. I wanted him to see me in shape, in perfect condition. If and when he saw me naked, I wanted him to be as turned on as I would be seeing him. I knew that the only way to do that was to keep running, keep pushing forward.

\*\*\*

"Hey, how are you feeling?" Autumn asked, as I headed into Ted's at five p.m. I had my regular shift with Devan, and I was very nervous about how the night was going to go. Was he going to talk to me, yell at me, and act like everything was normal?

When he came in, he was smiling … until he saw me. His smile instantly turned into a pout, and he walked into the other room. It was definitely not a good sign about how the night was going to go. I took a deep breath and did the only thing I could think of. I followed him. I increased my pace and went into the kitchen to find him.

He was leaning against the vegetable rack, taking full and deep breaths. He looked pretty upset. He looked over at me and spotted my watery eyes. He looked shocked that I was starting to cry. What did he expect me to do, smile as he walked away?

"You know what," I started, breathing in. Here it came … the ugly cry. My nemesis. "You have no right to be angry with me! I'm the one who was hurt in this situation! It's always me. I'm always fucking hurt. Every guy, including you, takes advantage—"

He silenced me with a hard, passionate kiss. He held my arms and brought me up, closer to his lips and his body. Oh, did I want him. I couldn't think about anything else but his lips and his hands on me. I wanted more. I needed more.

He broke the kiss and then kissed my cheeks, soft and gentle, so delicate. I realized quickly that he was quite literally "kissing away" my tears.

"I'm … " I exhaled, trying to speak. I couldn't breathe when he kissed me that way. His finger came to my lips, telling me to shush.

"Please, don't," he said. "Don't ruin the moment."

He walked away, and we went on with our night. It was pretty busy, so we worked hard together. I bussed tables. I brought out glasses, silverware, and ice. I replaced the full bus buckets with new, clean ones. I worked my ass off, creating a quicker turnover for the whole restaurant.

I watched Devan talk to customers, laugh while he

brought people drinks, and of course, flirt with every girl he could. I was a little jealous, but I tried to remind myself that we weren't together. He was the sexy bartender who could get with all the girls. I was just the busser.

When nine o'clock rolled around, I started cleaning up so I could leave. As I put away a few racks of glasses, Devan came up behind me.

"What are you doing tomorrow night?"

My mouth dropped open, and all of the color left my face. I was going to either cry, throw up, or pee my pants. "Um … "

"Come to a party with me. You were right; you were right about everything."

"I … " I took a deep breath. Was this actually happening? "I was right?"

He laughed and shook his head, opening his arms for me. I went into his arms and instantly relaxed. It felt so good, him holding me, protecting me, comforting me.

*I love you,* I thought instantly, without even thinking it through. The thought scared me just a tad, and I wondered if that could have been true. Did I love Devan? Could you love someone you barely knew?

I let go of him, and he walked away, turning for just a second to look at me again as he headed in the opposite direction. And just as he left, I realized what I'd done. I'd made two dates for the following night. I *never* got asked out on dates ... so, of course, the two times I did it was for the same night.

I stared up at the ceiling in awe and shook my head at God.

*Seriously?*

# Chapter Seven

I got out of work by nine thirty and called Frank on the way to my car.

"Hello?" Frank answered very quickly.

"Hey, Frank. It's Stacey! So, here's the thing. I forgot I had plans tomorrow night ..."

He laughed. "Don't lie, Stacey. I'm a big boy. If you don't want to go out with me, I can deal with it."

I shook my head, horrified. I really did want to go out with him—just not tomorrow! I wasn't going to ruin my chances with Devan by saying no!

"Seriously, tell me the truth."

"Can I tell you the whole truth, Frank? You won't get mad?" I asked.

"Obviously." He laughed a hearty, manly laugh. It was so sexy.

"I'm into this bartender I work with, and for some reason he asked me out for tomorrow night. I don't think he and I will work out, but I want to try anyway. I still want to see you. Just not tomorrow night." We were both laughing now.

"No shit?"

"Swear."

"Well, what are you doing tonight?" he asked, completely disregarding what I had just said about Devan. He was letting it slide.

"I just finished working."

"How long will it take you to get ready?"

I smiled wide. "Give me a half hour, and I'm your girl."

\*\*\*

"Can I please go out tonight?"

Danielle was all curled up in her bed with a glass of wine. "Can you be home at a reasonable time?" she asked, eyeing me up and down, checking my outfit. She looked me up and down. She scanned my black tank top and tight cheetah-print skirt. This outfit was definitely not my classiest. "Um, that outfit is pretty slutty."

My face fell instantly, and I wondered if that was why I had been raped—was it the outfit I wore that night? Had I asked for it to happen? I felt a lump in the back of my throat. I blinked back tears and took a deep breath.

"You should probably cover up a little bit," Danielle said. "But have fun."

I closed the door quickly and walked to the bathroom. I calmed myself down, pushing my thoughts of Mike away, and reapplied my mascara and eyeliner. As I finished putting on just a hint of blush, my phone vibrated.

```
Frank: Hey beautiful! ready?
```

I smiled a huge smile and texted back.

```
Stacey: I am :) Always ready for a
cute guy
Frank: Cute? Really? I prefer sexy.
But cute is okay I guess. I'll be
there in 5
```

I was starting to get nervous now. Frank was so

much funnier and cuter than I remembered. He was also right on time. Within five minutes, Frank was at my front door with one red rose. My jaw dropped as he handed it to me. Not only had Frank walked to my door to pick me up, but he had given me my favorite flower. Damn, was Frank amazing.

"Oh my gosh." I shook my head in awe. "You … you shouldn't have!"

"Nope. I should have," he said and walked inside. I went to the kitchen sink and filled a small, clear vase with water.

"Can I get you something to drink?"

"No thanks," he said with a smile. "I'm okay."

I tried to focus on the flowers now. I took out a knife and brought the blade a few inches in on the stem of the rose. I pushed down on the blade, and somehow, it slipped and my mind started spinning.

*Blood. Blood. Blood everywhere.*

"Stacey!"

I looked down at my hand, and there was the pain's creator: a long, thin gash in the center of my palm. For just a second, as I watched the blood flow out of my skin, there were absolutely no thought in my brain. I wasn't nervous for my date, and I had no negative thoughts in my mind. When the blood fell, I didn't feel anything—just the pain from the cut.

"I'm okay," I said, breathing in and out through my nose. Frank's arm came around me and brought me toward the sink. He turned the sink on and brought my hand toward the cold water. The sting was instant, as the water seared through my cut.

"Are you sure you're okay?" he asked, looking into my eyes. We were very close to each other. I realized that now. Our lips were only a few inches away.

"I'm … " I paused. I was okay. I mean, I definitely needed a very large bandage on my hand … but I was going to live. "Thank you." Timidly, I stepped away from his grip and looked through my medicine cabinet for bandages. I found one and secured it over my cut.

"I'm first-aid certified," he said, a huge smirk on his face. He was *so* cocky.

"I'm glad you are … I probably would have just stood there looking at all the blood."

He shook his head, understanding, and brought a wet paper towel to the counter, where he wiped up a few spots of blood. "You know what a great painkiller is?" he asked, moving closer to me now. He was so close. He was so cute. He was so … manly.

"Alcohol?"

"You got it, babe."

I popped three Advil, downed a large glass of water, and we both left in his Audi.

"So, where are you taking me?" I asked, rubbing the bandage on my hand. The cut really stung.

"A party in Louville. How does that sound?"

By the time we got to Louville (the closest island to Ridgefield), it was ten thirty, and I'd already downed three shots of Captain Morgan in his car. I was good and loose.

He took my hand as I stepped out of the car and walked me to the front door. Once inside, surrounding me was a group of about fifteen young, attractive college guys, all of whom were on some sports team in high school. I remembered their faces from basketball, football, and baseball games. Frank was on the baseball team all four years of high school, actually. He was pretty good.

"You are the ultimate jock," I whispered under my breath, for just Frank to hear. I was still holding the bottle of Captain and taking small, painful sips from the very large bottle.

"Hey, guys, remember Stacey?" Everyone looked at me, confused, like they didn't know how they knew me. Frank caught on to their confusion. "She sang at all the talent shows?" All the guys still looked confused. Frank laughed over to me and kept going. "She won Battle of the Bands all three years with her band?"

Frank was hysterical now, realizing none of these

guys would ever go to a talent show or Battle of the Bands.

"She got with that track guy Thomas Right, and he told *everyone* about how good it was?"

Everyone suddenly remembered me now and went on drinking. I looked up at Frank and smiled. He was too funny.

He took my hand and brought me to the dining room in the back of the house. The first thing I noticed about the room was the stench ... Weed was everywhere. A few guys were sitting around a table, rolling and smoking at the same time. One I knew from Battle of the Bands—he was a really good guitarist who was also on the tennis team—and the other two were soccer jocks. The guitarist smiled and gave me a big hug.

"Stacey Lorenzo ... master of Battle of the Bands. What's up?" I held on tight, loving the compliment. I also loved that someone I knew was here.

"I can't believe there's a fellow musician here," I joked. This was not our scene. "Nothing really, what about you?" Frank sat down next to one of the jocks. He seemed a little tense now that I was talking to the guitarist, but he didn't say anything. I could just tell by the hard facial expression that he was a little jealous.

"Nothing. I have a new band, though. You should hear us!"

I smiled, loving the idea … but not wanting to piss off Frank. "That sounds great. Maybe Frank and I will go check out the band together." I looked over at Frank with a smile, and he instantly lit up. He was such a boy.

"Definitely!"

The guitarist sat back down now, and I walked around to the other side of the table to be near Frank. There weren't any chairs left, so he pulled back in his seat and seated me in his lap.

I sat down willingly, trying to remind myself that he could handle my weight. *I'm not fat anymore. I'm not fat anymore. I'm not fat anymore.*

"You're so light, Stace," Frank said, leaning me back on his chest, my feet lifting to rest on the table. That literally was the best compliment he could have given me. *Stacey Lorenzo? Light? It almost wasn't possible.* I closed my mouth, forcing myself not to ask him, *Really? You're not suffocating right now?*

The guy next to me handed Frank a bowl and a lighter. Frank's body came around me just a bit tighter, and I leaned back into his chest. His right hand brought the bowl to my face. I put my lips around it.

"Breathe in, baby," he said, using his left hand to light the weed inside the bowl. I sucked in, and he took his finger off the carb hole on the side of the bowl as I sucked, taking it all in. All of the smoke rushed to the back of my throat and burned. I sucked in for as long as I could and then let the smoke go slowly.

*Whoa. What a rush.* I coughed for just a second and leaned back into Frank.

"You're so sexy," Frank whispered in my ear. My whole body responded to his words. My back arched, pushing my ass harder into his crotch. I could feel him up against my ass. I could make out the outline of his dick along my skin. He held on to my hips now and leaned his head on my shoulder.

I wanted him more than I ever thought I could. Frank and I were without a doubt beyond friends. After a few more hits, and a lot more flirting with Frank … I was ready. I wanted him to kiss me. I wanted him to touch me. I wanted him.

"Take me upstairs."

He didn't hesitate for a moment. Within a few seconds, he was leading me up the long stairwell toward a bedroom. It was crazy; I felt so alive at this moment. Weed and alcohol still on my breath, a hot guy on my arm *who wanted me* … I really was living. I was pushing my limits.

I wanted to now. Unlike with Mike, I had the control now, and I wanted to show Frank that I was the dominant one, that I was the one who would be calling the shots. Mike had taken something from me; with

Frank, I wanted to be the one to give it. I wanted to be able to say what I wanted and what my needs were.

I was halfway up the stairs when my hands came down to the bottom of my tank top. I lifted it off my body smoothly, exposing my black bra. I really didn't care if the other guys saw my body now. All I wanted was for Frank to see me.

His hands came around me from behind and held me back. He played around the edge of my skirt and then made patterns on the bottom of my stomach. His touch was surely teasing me.

His fingertips slid up my skin inch by inch, making me moan. Then he came to the back of my bra and unhooked it with ease. Within seconds, my bra was on the ground and his hands were filled with my breasts. His hands squeezed them, hard.

"You can strip for me anytime, baby." His hands came down to my skirt and slowly glided it off my body. I stepped out of it and quickly moved forward, up the stairs. I turned to face him where he stood, still at the center of the staircase, and made complete eye contact. My eyes stayed on his as my hands went down to my red lace panties. I leaned over and pulled them off, stepping out of them and leaving them on the floor.

I was standing there, naked. Just looking at Frank. Just wanting Frank. And I could tell by the way he was looking at me that he wanted me—he might have even thought I was beautiful.

His hands were now on his shirt, which he eased off of his body. Damn, he looked good. Frank was a man in all senses of the word; he was a bulging man and small pockets of hair covered his tan, soft skin. His shoulders were broad, but his stomach wasn't perfect. He had pecs that rose slightly from his well-built chest, but a small pocket of fat filled the bottom of his stomach. The extra pounds seemed to work for him, though. It was sexy.

He tossed his shirt at me, and it hit my body and fell to the floor. I giggled as he smiled up at me. His pants and boxers came off in one sweep. We were both naked in the stairwell, with all of our clothes surrounding us. It was so sexy, dangerous, and fun, all at the same time.

He walked toward me now with a wicked grin. I ran down the small hallway, knowing he would follow me into the bedroom. I could hear him laughing, and his footsteps on the wood floor.

"You can't outrun me, beautiful." He was behind me now. He swung me around and brought his lips to mine. He was touching everywhere. Except the wetness between my legs. I needed his hands there. He walked me backward toward the bed and laid me down.

Before I knew it, his hands were pushing me up on

the bed so my head was on the pillow.

"Lay back and relax," he said. I could see his faint smile in the dim hallway light, and then it was out of view. I couldn't see him, but I could without a doubt feel him. He was licking down my torso slowly, teasingly, and then he was there. His tongue, his fingers were inside me. Gliding in and out.

"I … " I was really moaning now, not knowing if I could handle this. Something was building inside me … something I'd never felt before. "I've never … "

"Had an orgasm?" He paused for just a moment, and then went back to what he was doing. His tongue slipped inside, and I screamed. I was oh so close, everything was rushing to my head, and my whole body felt numb. I couldn't control anything.

I took a deep breath, trying to control the urge to let go … and then I suddenly felt nauseous. I felt clammy and weird. My stomach hurt. Before I knew it, I was gagging.

"Whoa, Stacey!"

My head was over the bed now, and I was purging everything. Calories, food, alcohol was pouring from my mouth, onto the floor. Tears filled my eyes as I gagged yet again and threw up the last bit of alcohol.

"Stacey! Are you okay?"

I was hysterical now. This was a different kind of

throwing up. When I forced myself, I was the one in control. I knew when it would start and stop. But this sort of throwing up was not controlled. This was my body's decision, not my own.

"I feel awful," I said, hiccupping. I was doing the ugly cry. I really just wanted to go home now.

"Baby, I'm sorry. Let me get your clothes. I'll clean this up." Frank walked out of the bedroom as I got out of the bed, making sure to dodge the vomit. I really needed to get out of here. The smell of vomit was revolting.

He came back into the room and turned the light on. Frank had all our clothes in his hands and dropped them on the ground. When he dropped the clothes, I saw his dick. He was still so hard. I grabbed my panties first and slipped them on quickly. I didn't want him to see me naked in such a bright room.

"Frank, I'm so sorry," I cried, wiping tears from my eyes.

"Stacey, we've all been there." I put on my clothes as Frank watched. His whole body responded as I put my bra on and my jeans. Even though I had just thrown up while he was going down on me … he still wanted me.

"I'm going to clean this up," I said, walking toward the bathroom. I got a lot of paper towels and the garbage can. I was still crying as I kneeled down on the floor and started cleaning it up. Frank came beside me now (with his shirt off) and took some paper towels in his hand. He was actually helping me clean up my vomit.

"Don't cry, Stacey," he said, throwing paper towels into the waste bin. All we needed to do was wash the floor with some water and Lysol. I found some Lysol under the sink and got to work.

"I feel so bad. I can't believe this just happened," I said, wiping my nose with my forearm.

"I can. Do you know how many times I've thrown up after drinking?" He smiled over at me and stood up so he could put his shirt on. I rubbed a little more Lysol onto the floor.

"Not while a girl was blowing you, though!"

He laughed, and I sighed. I brought the trash back into the bathroom and flushed everything down the toilet, then washed out the bin with some Lysol. I went to the sink next and washed my hands clean.

His hands came around me, and he hugged me from behind.

"You are so beautiful. That was amazing. And yeah, it was short lived, and I wish we had done more, Stacey. But you throwing up mid-hookup is better than not hooking up with you at all. You have no idea how amazing you are, do you?" His lips came just an inch from mine, and I shook my head.

"Don't kiss me; I just threw up, remember?" I said, giggling.

"Oh, right." He searched in his jeans for something and pulled out a piece of gum.

"Here, chew that. I'll get you some water, and then I'll drive you home," he said, hugging me. "I missed you."

"I missed you too, Frank."

"Are you going to forget about me?" he asked, looking down at me and holding me closer.

"How could I? I sliced my hand in front of you, and I threw up while you went down on me. Who could forget that?" We both laughed and headed downstairs hand in hand.

# Chapter Eight

The next morning, I woke up with a severe headache and found texts from Devan, Clare, my mom, and Frank. I also had twelve missed calls from Clare.

Devan: Hey, I'll pick you up at 9 tonight?

Clare: WAY TO ANSWER YOUR PHONE LAST NIGHT. I HAD TO CALL YOUR SISTER TO SEE IF YOU WERE ALIVE. Hate you. Hate you. Hate you. Call me when you wake up ... <3

Mom: Good morning, baby! I hope you have been keeping in touch with

your father better than you have with
me, young lady.

Frank: Good morning beautiful :)


I read all the messages, each one putting an even
bigger smile on my face. I had a date tonight with
Devan, and Frank had been awesome the night before!

I texted both of my parents at the request of my
mother to check in. That wasn't exactly a fun aspect of
my day, but it was definitely necessary.

"Hello?" She answered on the first ring.

"Hi. I'm sorry I forgot to text you last night. I sort
of passed out on the way home."

"I still hate you," she said, laughing at my stupidity.
"What happened last night?"

"Frank is fucking awesome. But it didn't go very
well. I'm pretty sure he thinks I'm insane."

"Why?"

"Because I cut myself while cutting flowers, and he
basically had to calm me down and dress my wound."
We both laughed at that. "And then we had the most
insane stripping make-out session on the stairs, and
when we got to the bedroom he went down on me …
and I was about to orgasm but instead of finally having
my big moment, I threw up."

"ON HIM?" she screamed into the phone, making

me hold the cell away from my ear.

"No, the floor. Thank God!" We were both laughing hysterically now. It really was funny. My sexual experiences really weren't normal.

"I miss you," she said once our laughing died down.

"I miss you, too," I said. "Come over and we can go for a long walk and talk. I'll even make you lunch."

"That sounds great."

"I'll see you in fifteen." We hung up quickly, and then I proceeded to text back the boys I was oh-so-eager to talk to. I really liked both of them.

```
Stacey: Yeah Devan, 9 sounds great
Stacey: Hey Frank! I'm surprised
you didn't go running for the hills
after what happened last night!
```

All of the throwing up and cuts aside, last night was pretty amazing. I really liked Frank and the way he made me feel. He had taken me to a party where all of his friends were, no problem. Plus, he had still wanted to take me out even though I told him the truth about Devan. Beyond all of that, he had taken care of me when I needed him. He had made me feel loved, safe, and protected.

Devan made my whole body shake and my face

flush. With us, there was just an easy connection. Our relationship was sexual and emotional at the same time. Could I pass up a guy like Devan, who made my sexual being come alive, to be with a normal guy like Frank? Frank was emotional and sensitive, but he was almost too nice, too perfect. I needed a spark, and Mr. Teddy Bear definitely did not give me one. But, despite my reservations, I really wanted to give him a chance.

Frank: Of course not!

Stacey: Good, I'm glad because I miss you

Frank: You do?

Stacey: Nope. I was jk

Frank: LOL YOU SO TOTALLY MISS ME

Stacey: Maybe you're right. I do. When are you going back to school?

Frank: Monday

Frank: Tomorrow night. Dinner. You and I. Say yes.

Stacey: Yes!

\*\*\*

At nine o'clock, I was ready. Clare and I had gone on a very long walk and then watched a Rom-Com. I had showered, straightened my hair, put on makeup, and Clare and Danielle helped me pick out my outfit. We decided on jean shorts and a tank top paired with my favorite stilettos. Casual and dressy at the same time. At around nine fifteen, Devan texted me that he was there, and I headed out the door. He was in his old, beat-up Subaru.

I got in the car. He was smiling ear to ear as I fastened my seatbelt. He leaned over, and within seconds he brought his mouth toward mine. It was hard and sexy. He was sexy and skilled. He was skilled and badass.

"Whoa," I said, as his tongue came out of my mouth and he pulled away. He laughed and brushed his hands through his beautiful red hair. I tried to breathe.

The kiss was amazing, as always, but something about it felt rushed. Forced. Like he was trying to prove something to me. I stared at him as he put on his Red Sox hat … and everything seemed normal with him. He was in jeans and a T-shirt, and his usual baseball cap.

"I … I missed you," I said, my voice shaking.

"I missed you too, sexy."

"Is everything okay?" I asked as we headed out of

my neighborhood. He was driving very fast, scaring me just a tad.

"Yeah, everything's cool." His hand moved from my hand to my leg, then higher up my thigh. My legs tingled; he gave me goosebumps. I couldn't believe how forward he was being. Not only had he kissed me (with tongue!) just seconds after I'd sat in the passenger seat, but his hand was just inches from my panties. The worst part was I totally liked it.

Devan blared Drake, and we headed toward his friend's house. His hand was still on my leg, and it was still turning me on. I mean, it was forward … but why did I care? Devan was touching me. Devan. I'd take what I could get.

"Ready?" Devan asked as we parked down the street from his friend's house. He didn't help me get out of the car as Frank had, but he took my hand before we headed through the door. As I walked through the door, I was completely and utterly shocked. No one even turned their head to look at me, and no one was talking.

There were five couples on the floor, hooking up in separate corners of the room. There was a large group of people in a circle, all surrounding a large, glass coffee table.

Devan and I walked toward the table, and I finally

realized why they were all surrounding the table. All over it was a white, powdery substance, which Devan confirmed was cocaine.

"Oh, shit," I whispered, looking over at Devan. He didn't seem to mind. This was obviously a normal sight for him. He seemed annoyed that I cared, actually, not that people were doing coke. He disregarded my reaction and walked me toward the table.

"Hey, guys, who has alcohol?" Devan asked softly. It was eerily quiet and creepy in the house. I really didn't feel comfortable. This wasn't my crowd at all. I also wondered if that's why Devan was being so weird in the car … Was he possibly high on cocaine?

A boy across from us handed Devan a bottle of vodka. Devan passed the bottle to me, and I took a long, hard swig. I didn't even have anything to chase it with, and I still had a hangover from the night before. What I was doing was without a doubt a bad idea, but I didn't really care. Devan was being really shady, and his friends were weird as hell. The vodka was the only thing that could possibly break the ice.

I took another swig, ignoring my sudden urge to vomit as a boy next to Devan handed him a joint. He took a hit, slowly, calmly, like he'd done it a million times, and then handed it over to me. I brought the joint to my lips and slowly took all of the smoke into my lungs. I coughed my way through the exhale like an amateur.

The guy next to me pointed to the cocaine as if to say I could try it. Cocaine was an actual drug, unlike marijuana. I mean sure, I handed weed well, but Cocaine was so much stronger. Would I have a similar tolerance to this drug? The next thought that came to my mind was what the hell did I have to lose? I wasn't driving, and I'd never tried it before. And more than anything, I knew that if I was on a drug like that, there was no way I'd be thinking about Mike, my weight, or my life at all. I looked to Devan, questioning whether I should or not. He nodded, so I took a deep breath and knelt down in front of the table.

I took the dollar bill sitting on the table and brought it to my nose. I breathed deeply and snorted the line of cocaine into my nostril. The burning that came after that one inhalation was horrendous. Tears filled my eyes, and they fell down my cheeks. I held on to the table tight and stood back up, next to Devan. He took my hand, obviously understanding that snorting hurt. He didn't say anything, but I could tell he cared.

Around the circle, you didn't talk. You focused on getting fucked up. It was like clockwork. Long, hard swig of vodka. Slow, painful hit of weed. Harsh, intense snort of cocaine.

I was on my fourth swig of vodka, third hit of weed, and second line of coke when I realized that I needed to slow down. I had never been this fucked up in my life. The only reason I was standing was because Devan's hands were literally holding me up. Plus, I couldn't stop sniffing. My nose was still burning and nothing I did made it feel better.

Devan was still being weird. He was barely talking, along with all of the other people at the party. Plus, he was totally acting like he didn't give a shit that I was there. He didn't introduce me to his friends. He didn't even acknowledge me unless I looked like I was going to fall.

My phone vibrated in my pocket.

```
Frank: Hey what are you doing?
Stacey: Atttttta party d :) Frankyy
rpoo
Frank: You're so drunk.
Stacey: NIEP ... nopee . Coke. Weed.
Frank: Cocaine? are you okay?
Stacey: Sortaaof
Frank: Why don't I pick you up?
Stacey: cantt. Devyy poo would be
maddy poo
```

Devan looked down and noticed I was texting. He seemed annoyed as I swayed to one side. I totally was not doing well. I really needed to sit down.

"Who's Frank?" Devan asked, looking at my text.

"I went on a date with him last night," I said, proud of myself that I could make out the words. I swayed once more, but this time didn't chance it. I held on to Devan's shoulders, looking into those big blue eyes of his.

He'd had twice the amount of alcohol, weed, and lines that I had, and yet he seemed totally fine. He put his arms around me protectively. His hands grazed the top of my butt, and then he pushed his luck by taking his hands all the way down, squeezing my full ass with his hands.

"Let's get out of here," he said, motioning for the bedroom just down the hall.

"I can't walk," I said, laughing.

He smiled at me, acting more like himself now. "I carried you once, I can carry you again." His arms came around my legs and back and lifted me effortlessly. This time, I didn't have a concussion, but he was still my protector. He had been weird most of the night, but right when he touched me, all of the problems seemed to melt away.

"Blow me," he said, sitting me down on the bed

and standing in front of me.

"Umm … " I said, trying to focus. Had he really just done this to me? He got me fucked up, carried me into a bedroom, and ordered me to blow him? *Really?*

I looked down at his jeans and could see the faint outline of his erection. *Had I really done that to him? Had I turned him on just by being in his presence?* The thought of Devan getting hard from me … boring Stacey Lorenzo … well, that changed my mind.

"Get on the bed," I said, trying my hardest not to sway from side to side as I got up from the bed for just a second as he took my spot. The twin bed was small, but it was just big enough for the two of us. I liked that.

My head spun, and I closed my eyes, trying to stop the spinning of the bedroom around me. Everything was moving, like a spinning top, and it wouldn't stop.

Devan squeezed my hand, obviously impatient and wanting me to begin. I opened my eyes at his cue, and my hands came to his shirt. I stripped it off. He closed his eyes now, as I kissed him. It was a quick, chaste kiss, but the rest was all sexual. I kissed down his torso and found his happy trail. That's when I started pulling off his jeans and his navy-blue boxers.

I used my hands first, exploring all of him.

I couldn't control myself any longer, couldn't wait for his reaction anymore, so I brought my lips down, teasing him. I started from the top and worked my way down.

He was moaning again. It was amazing how much his pleasure affected me. I was so wet now, all because he was moaning for me, whispering my name, wanting more.

His whole body clenched, along with his hands in my hair as I took him as far as I could. He was all in now; he was brushing up against the back of my throat.

I was racing to his finish line now. He was screaming, loud and powerful. I loved that I was making this happen. I was doing this to him.

He exploded inside my mouth. There was a lot more than I expected, and it glazed the back of my throat. I swallowed it as quickly as I could, trying to get the salty taste out of my mouth.

His eyes locked on mine, and he grinned wide.

"That was amazing, Stacey." He kissed me now, taking my ass in his hands. "Take your clothes off," he said, motioning for me to stand.

*Headrush.* I stumbled on the floor and fell into the wall. Those heels were really killing me.

"Shit," I said, laughing, and brought my hands down to my tank top to unhook my black Victoria's Secret bra. My boobs were already aroused. My nipples were elongated, and my breasts were full.

I unzipped my shorts and flung off my stilettos. *Fuck them.* I took my cell out of the jeans pocket and put it on top of the pile. I slowly pulled down my panties, thanking the Lord that the lights were off and he could only barely see me from the streetlights.

He pulled me down to the bed, and he got on top. His lips were on mine, and then his tongue was in my mouth and then working down my body. His hands, tongue, lips ... they were everywhere. And every touch, every nibble, every caress made me want to combust. This kid fucked me from the inside out. I couldn't believe the way he made my body react.

"Oh my God," was all I could say ... over and over as his hands fucked me. First it was his finger, stroking me gently, and then he was bringing more than one inside me.

It was intense and crazy as he kept pushing them inside. This didn't hurt like it had with Mike. With Devan, I was so wet and so into it. It wasn't forced or rushed. It was sexy as hell.

Everything was spinning. My mind, my head, my heart. I was so close to orgasm, I could feel the four walls crashing around me and my whole body stalling. I could feel it within my reach, and that scared me. I'd never had an orgasm in my life. I had never experienced it, and I wasn't sure if I wanted Devan to be the first guy to do that to me. Could I trust him to make me feel the things I never had?

If Devan got me off, I would want to hook up with him a lot … and there was a large chance he wouldn't even talk to me in the morning. This was Devan we were talking about: he wasn't a man of his word and I barely trusted him.

So I faked it. I screamed. It was sexy and loud. I did my best to make it look real by tensing up and squirming, too. Devan looked at me and smiled. He totally bought it.

"You are so sexy," he said, kissing my lower lip and sucking on it. I kissed him back, wanting him to hold me like this forever.

"Thank you," I said, not knowing what else to say. "We should probably get back." I looked at the clock.

"Yeah, why don't we get you home," he said, starting to get off me and put his clothes back on. I stood up, searching for my panties, and slipped them on in the darkness. "Watch your eyes," Devan said, and then switched on the lights.

"Stacey … " he said slowly. "Your nose is bleeding." He gave me some tissues and started wiping the blood off my hands and face. I hadn't even noticed it was bleeding. Apparently, using cocaine could make your nose bleed. As he was cleaning my hand, he saw the wound from the night with Frank.

"What happened to your hand?" he asked as I searched for my bra. I found it underneath the bed.

"I cut myself yesterday while cutting flowers." I shrugged. Why did he care?

"What about those?" he asked, walking toward me. He had on all his clothes now, and he pointed to the thin, red scars running over the surface of my stomach.

"I ... " I started, trying to find a good excuse. I was still fucked up. The words wouldn't come to me. "I don't know," was all I could come up with. His face seemed pained at first, truly upset, but then his emotion changed to anger and his frown hardened into a thin line.

"That's such a fucking lie."

"I'm not lying," I whispered. I didn't like when he got angry with me in general, but now that Mike had happened, guys getting angry made me fear for my safety. Guys could hurt me.

"Yes, you are," he said, his face red.

"Stop, Devan," I said, hoping to God he'd drop the subject. For Christ's sake, if I wanted to talk to him, I would have already.

"Why are you cutting yourself?" he asked, coming closer to me. He was holding me now. His protective arms were around my shoulders. He was the man. I was the little girl.

"Back off, Devan," I spoke into his chest.

"It's about that guy, isn't it?" he asked, looking down at me. "You're cutting because that guy raped you."

# Chapter Nine

I woke up the next morning with a protruding stomach and a severe headache. I hadn't thrown up since drinking with Devan, so I knew that throwing up was the first thing on the agenda, and then I had to eat healthier and go on an insane workout. Usually working out took away my stomach.

By twelve o'clock, I had gone on a two-hour run (let's be honest, it was a jog) … never stopping! I felt like gold as I headed into the house. I was soaked from head to toe in sweat. My face was beet-red from the activity. It was obvious how hard I'd worked.

"Hey, how was the workout?" Danielle asked as I got a glass of water in the kitchen. She was making

herself a bagel with cream cheese. I wanted one too…
a nice big bagel smothered in peanut butter with
sliced banana on top. Before I reached for the bag of
bagels that she was putting away, I touched my lower
stomach … reminding myself right where that bagel
would go. Right to my lower belly that I *hated* more
than anything else in the whole world.

I gulped down some water.

"It was really good, actually. Two hours. I ran slow,
though."

Her mouth was completely open in shock. "You
just ran for two hours?"

"Yes," I said, smiling. She was right. That was a
pretty awesome accomplishment. I must have burned a
lot of calories. "Pretty awesome, right?"

"Yes, very awesome."

"So, what are you up to today?" I went to the fruit
bowl and pulled out a banana.

"I'm going to go to the mall. How do you feel
about tagging along?" she asked, taking a big bite of
her bagel. I exhaled. *Think about skinny jeans. You
don't need the bagel. Think about skinny jeans.*

"Yes, I'd love to. That sounds awesome!"

After a quick shower, a check of the scale, and a
change of clothes, I was ready … and looking pretty
damn good. I decided I was totally going to wear the

same outfit on my date with Frank.

"I love your dress," Danielle said, eyeing me up and down. It was definitely cute. White. Short. Sexy *and* cute.

"Thank you."

We got into the car and headed toward the bank so I could take out some of the money I'd recently deposited. After getting money, and a quick frozen yogurt (I figured it was okay, as I only had a banana for breakfast), and two large waters, we headed out to the mall.

"You know, I really missed you. I feel like we've both been doing our own thing since Mom left," Danielle said in the lull between us singing country songs. I looked over to my sister, a little shocked. Unlike my eldest sister, Kara, Danielle wasn't one to be sentimental. Danielle was like Clare in that way. Kara and I were the open ones.

"I missed you, too."

Danielle changed the radio station to another country station. I didn't mind country when I was with Danielle, because I knew she loved it ... and honestly, it was fun to listen to. I liked to listen to all genres every once in a while.

"You really scared me. You know that, right?"

Since that night, we hadn't really talked about why

I passed out, or how we'd felt about the whole ordeal. I didn't think she would bring it up. Danielle and I did fun things together a lot, but we didn't have deep conversations with each other.

"I'm sorry," I said, putting my head down.

"Are you going to tell me what happened that day?" She looked over at me for a second and then merged her way onto the highway.

"Do I have to?" I really didn't want to talk about this with her. I wasn't ready to talk about my anxiety, about my weight. I didn't want to have to explain myself to my sister, who surely wouldn't understand what I was going through. I would be sent right to counseling, or worse, the loony bin.

"No, but when you're ready … I'm here to talk."

\*\*\*

I ran through the door and sprinted straight to my bathroom when we got home. I needed to put on makeup, straighten my hair, and switch out my flip-flops for heels. I wasn't sure where we were going, but I figured if I was wearing a sundress and heels I would be ready for anything.

"I can't believe you're going on a first date with Frank," Danielle said, standing in the doorway of the bathroom, watching me put on some eyeliner. "He's not your type at all; he's actually a nice person."

"Shut up. Not every guy I date's an asshole." She chuckled to herself. "And it's technically date number two," I added, smiling over at her.

"Um, when was the first one?"

I decided on blue eyeshadow. A dark navy blue that would accentuate my hazel-brown eyes. Something that popped.

"The first one?" I thought aloud, thinking back to my very intense hookup with him … with all of my clothes off. "Like, a few days ago."

"How was it?" she asked, coming into the bathroom to sit on the toilet seat.

"Actually, it ended kind of shitty."

"Why?"

"Well, we hooked up, and I threw up like midway through."

Danielle shook her head and brought her hands to her ears. "OH MY GOD!" she screamed, bouncing off the toilet seat. Have I mentioned that she's protective? Well, she is. Like an older brother. "La la la!" she sang. She really didn't like hearing about me getting with guys. "I don't want to know!" She danced away from the bathroom and down the stairs.

"You're just jealous!" I sang back, laughing and continuing with my makeup. I looked really put together. My makeup looked really edgy and cool, but my dress was very preppy. I had the perfect mix. I liked it that way, actually; I liked bringing both of my styles into the equation.

I could pull both styles off, because of my band (the edgy part) and because I went to Ridgefield High (aka the preppy capital of the world). So instead of being like everyone else and sticking to one style … I chose to be myself and be both. Preppy with a slight edge. Sexy and classy.

"Frank's here!" Danielle called from downstairs. I stared at my reflection in the mirror, exhaling. They were chatting downstairs, but I couldn't quite make out what it was about.

"Coming!" I called, slipping on my jean jacket and heading downstairs.

"Hey, you," I said, smiling down at him. There he was. All smiles. All perfection. All Frank.

"Oh, hey," he said. I headed toward him, and, of course, tripped on my very last step. He didn't catch me romantically, didn't even try to help actually … he just watched as I fell oh-so-gracefully on my face.

"I think I give you bad luck," Frank said, kneeling

down beside me and picking me up by my shoulders.

I laughed, shaking my head. Internally, I was freaking. *Don't cry. Don't cry. Don't cry.* I needed to do whatever was necessary not to do the ugly cry. "I think so too," I said, looking up at Danielle.

She looked shocked and embarrassed for me all at the same time. "That was hysterical," she said, cracking up. I swatted her arm playfully, grabbed my clutch on the table, and took Frank's arm. Even though I'd literally started the night out with a bang, I was determined to have a good time. I was a clumsy loser, but I looked hot tonight. I really did.

"How do you always seem to keep me on my toes?" Frank said, walking me to his car. He opened the door for me.

"You always seem to keep me *off* my toes, and on the floor."

He got into the car quickly, in his cute blue jeans and pink polo shirt. He looked like a gentleman. Put together. Sweet. I was excited as hell.

"Where do you want to go?" Frank asked, smiling over at me as we headed out of the neighborhood.

"I don't care," I said. "Just not—" I started, just as Frank opened up his cute, adorable mouth.

"What about Ted's?" he asked. Just the place I didn't want to go. I had eaten there so often *and* there was a chance Devan was working.

Devan … strong, beautiful, sexy Devan, with whom I had had an awesome evening the night before. I didn't want to be there with Frank … I wanted to be with Devan, who had proved to me that he really did care about me. He asked me questions about my problems. he wanted to know what was wrong.

I looked over to Frank, who was smiling over at me, telling me to buckle up. I really couldn't do this. I didn't care about him. I was going to compare him to Devan the whole night, and that wasn't fair to Frank. He was trying so hard, he was going to pay for dinner, and he was being a really sweet, nice guy to me. He didn't deserve my bullshit, and he didn't need my baggage.

"Frank." I brought my hand to his on the center console. His eyes reached mine and held. "Can you turn around, please?"

"Why?" he said, pulling the car over to the side of the road.

"I can't do this."

Frank put the car in park and positioned himself so that he was facing me.

"What?"

"I don't think I'm into this like you are. And I don't know why." For some reason, I started crying.

The ugly-cry switch went on, and I poured my heart out. "I've been going through a lot, and I hate this guy Devan, but I also love him. And you … you're just … wonderful."

Frank was holding me, his strong arms wrapped tight around me. I was at peace. I felt calm. That was the problem, though. I didn't feel flustered, or sexually charged, or afraid of getting hurt. I felt calm. I should've felt much more than just calm.

"I'm really confused. Please, try to calm down," Frank said, rubbing my back.

I paused for a long time, letting Frank "shush" me and say the occasional "There, there." I let him console me. I let him hold me until I calmed down, and then I spoke the only two sentences that I could come up with.

"I don't deserve you. And I have emotional baggage."

"What emotional baggage?" he asked, letting go of me and looking into my watery eyes.

Was I going to tell Frank about my long-standing issue with my weight? Was I going to tell Frank that I'd been raped, only making my self-esteem a bigger problem? Was I going to tell Frank that the only time I didn't feel alone was when I was drunk, high, or hooking up with a guy?

I had told enough people about the rape, and I really didn't want anyone else knowing. Frank and I were friends, but we weren't best friends. We definitely weren't lovers, either. There was no reason to go into my sob story. It sure as hell wouldn't make me feel better.

"Please, just take me home."

\*\*\*

When I got to the house, I checked in with Danielle. I knew I had to lie because I didn't want to tell her what happened. She would think I was crazy for picking Devan over Frank.

"I'm home. Frank didn't feel well and threw up on the side of the road."

"That seems to be a pattern in your relationship."

I frowned. "Guess so." I shut the door and headed to the refrigerator. I hadn't eaten dinner, so I figured I could squeeze in a few calories. I was hungry; I deserved the dinner.

In the fridge was a lot of strawberry Greek yogurt, fruit, and meats—steak, pork chops, and chicken— that I could cook for myself. If I grilled chicken and put it atop some romaine lettuce with cucumbers and tomatoes, I would have a healthy, satisfying dinner. Protein and vegetables. Not too many calories, but just enough.

I made the dish quickly and ate it in front of the TV. *Grey's Anatomy* reruns made my world go round. Well, hot doctors having hot sex with each other made my world go round ... but, ya know, there was no need to be technical.

By the end of the show, it was dark out and my meal was finished. Five pieces of chicken and a salad later, I was still hungry. My stomach was growling, and my mind was focused on one thing: chocolate. So I did what I knew best. I plugged in my iPod, turned to an all-Taylor Swift playlist, and baked myself a chocolate cake.

Sugar, flour, eggs, and vanilla ... I threw some things together, screaming along with Taylor to *Mean*. I tried the batter, so I knew it was fantastic. Within an hour and a half, the cake was baked, cooled, and ready for the icing. I made my favorite mocha-bean icing and slathered it on the cake. It really did look great, but to make it look even better, I finished it off with a layer of milk chocolate chips.

I took a few pictures, sending one to Danielle, Kara, Fred, my mom, Dad, and Clare, of course, and then decided I couldn't wait any longer. I took out a plate and a large glass of skim milk and sliced a very large slice of cake.

*Mmm.* The fork came to my lips, and I took the food into my mouth. It was so chocolaty, so mocha, so good. It went down easy. It made me feel charged, energized, and for some reason … loved. The food made me feel better. It was one of the few ways I could shut out my feelings.

"WHERE'S THE CAKE?" Danielle screamed, bounding down the stairs. She'd seen the picture I'd sent her, obviously. Like the rest of the family, Danielle was a big fan of my baked goods. I laughed, taking the last bite of my slice and then a quick gulp of milk.

"It's right here."

"Thank God! My prayers have been answered," Danielle said, doing the same thing I had done: plate, milk, cake. "I love you."

She headed up the stairs to her bedroom with plate and glass in hand as I contemplated my next move. Put the dish away? Put the glass away? Or have another slice? I mean, I hadn't eaten much that day. I had run for two hours. Plus, I could always do an extra-hard workout in the morning or cut back on the calories tomorrow.

The second piece of cake won. I wanted the

cake. I wanted the chocolate. I wanted the feeling of security that it gave me. Food was the answer to all my problems. I could eat; it would calm the feelings of anxiety.

I finished off the second piece quickly and ended up cutting a third. As I finished, I felt more and more guilty, so I called it a night. I put everything in the dishwasher and headed upstairs; I needed a shower. I stripped off my dress, exposing my strapless bra and lace panties … and my fat stomach. It was so large, so grotesque, so scary. Had three pieces of cake really created that? Was that possible?

My stomach was definitely bigger. My thighs were bigger. My arms were bigger. My face was bigger. My boobs were bigger. My ass was bigger. Everything was bigger. So I did what I had to do to take it away—I leaned over the toilet, gagging out all of my calories and relieving the little patch of fat at the bottom of my stomach.

I stepped into the shower and took out the soap. I scrubbed my face, my arms, my legs, my stomach, making sure to hit every contour of my skin. Every place that could have even a crumb of chocolate on it, I scrubbed. I didn't want to remember that I'd actually eaten three pieces of chocolate cake just because I had a few problems. And then I threw up every morsel of food in my stomach? Why was I so fucked up?

I lathered shaving cream on my legs and started shaving away every bit of hair. I did the same with my armpits. As I shaved, I looked at the back of the razor. The sharp edge wasn't attached to the plastic. It could be taken out. So, I took it out and examined it. It was gray, sharp, about three inches long, and super thin.

I felt its sharpness against my finger … It could definitely do some damage. I could run this thin, rigid object against my white skin, and it would turn red. I could make myself bleed.

I knelt down on the floor, trying to find a good spot to try it out on. My arm was too open to the public. My stomach was used all too often. My legs though … they were rarely seen and I'd never cut them before. They were the perfect spot.

I sat in the tile shower and stared down at my flesh. I brought the blade to my skin and pressed down hard, harder until it pierced. I dragged the razor over my skin, making the cut deeper and thicker. The cut ran from about six inches above my kneecap to the top of my thigh.

As I continued to slice my skin, my mind cleared. My heart stopped beating for just a second … and everything went quiet. My thoughts. My surroundings. I couldn't even hear the water hitting the tile.

I stopped thinking about Mike, his fingers that were forever on my skin. I stopped thinking about the way I'd treated Frank, one of the only sweet guys who had ever taken me out on a date. I stopped thinking about the fact that I had to stick my fingers down my throat to confront my problems. Everything paused.

For about ten seconds, it was just me, the blade, and the blood flowing down the tile to the drain.

# Chapter Ten

Devan texted me that night, for the first time since I'd last seen him. We hadn't talked much on the way home about the cutting he'd seen on my stomach; I didn't trust him enough to talk to him about my problems.

He was hot and cold—that was the only part of him that was consistent. He didn't want me. He wanted me. He hated me. He loved me. He wanted to fuck me. He didn't. I couldn't fucking deal with his mood swings and changes of heart anymore.

```
Devan: Hey, please talk to me
Stacey: no
```

```
Devan: ... You technically just did
lol
Stacey: I hate you lol
```

I had sworn to myself that I wasn't going to tell Devan anything, but for some reason he was making me feel comfortable enough to talk to him about this.

```
Devan: We both know that's not true
Stacey: Don't be cocky. I don't
like you as much as you assume I do.
```

I checked my phone almost every thirty seconds or so until I fell asleep, but when I woke up, he still hadn't responded. He'd given up on me.

Why wasn't he answering? Was he mad at me? Did he really believe me when I said I didn't like him very much? I was *obviously* lying. He didn't believe that, did he? I was so nervous, staring up at my ceiling, wondering what to do ... and then I made a decision. I was going to call him.

"Hello?" Devan answered on the first ring. He sounded very tense, almost angry. Behind him, I could hear the engine of a car and the rush of wind.

"Hey," I said timidly. I was regretting my decision to call him. He totally thought I was insane. I was bothering him. "It's me."

"So it is," he said shortly. "I thought you hated me." He was getting straight to the point.

"You seem angry," was the only response I could come up with. I had a thing for pointing out the obvious.

"Angry? Nope. Confused as hell is more like it." He was confused? About me? *Good.* He deserved it. My whole life was fucking confusion.

"Why?"

"Damn it, Stacey." His voice was growing angrier by the minute. "Why the fuck are you hurting yourself? That guy's a jerk. Press charges or get the fuck over it, but don't use a blade to confront your problems." My mouth dropped open, and my eyes started to tear. I felt like I had just been kicked in the teeth. I drew in a deep breath, loud enough that he could hear, and paused. I couldn't form words. Was he really this much of an insensitive bastard?

He swore again under his breath, obviously realizing what he'd just said. But his apology wasn't going to make a difference. He was a jerk. He was an asshole jerk. He was a douchebag asshole jerk. Oh, and a loser. So yes … that made him a loser, douchebag, asshole jerk.

"I'm sorry, Stacey. I'm sorry." He kept apologizing, but I zoned out. All I could hear in my head was "Get the fuck over it" … like it was that easy. Was he fucking dumb? I wasn't Superwoman. I had feelings. Sure, I dealt with them in a way that people didn't understand, but it wasn't unheard of. It was actually very common in teenage girls. I wasn't crazy. I was just going through a rough patch.

"I … " He was still apologizing as I finally spoke. "I hate … " I sobbed into the phone freely. I didn't care if he heard me cry. "I hate you."

For thirty seconds or more, neither of us spoke. I was crying, he was breathing. I heard him sigh. I could imagine him in his car. His phone would be on speaker in the center console, and his left hand (the one not on the wheel) would come to his forehead, and he'd quietly wonder, *What have I done?*

"I'm not kidding," I said finally, breaking the silence. My voice cracked on "kidding," and another sob broke out.

"Please don't cry." he sighed, his tone softer now, sweeter. He was turning back into the Devan I loved.

"I can't help it," I whispered, hiccupping at the end of the sentence. I always hiccupped when I cried. I had no idea why.

"I'm sorry I said that that way." He was searching for the perfect words. I could tell. "I have a really hard time interacting with people. Especially people who are doing things I don't understand."

"You don't understand. That's no reason to berate me." I smiled at myself. I may have seemed weak, but I still stuck up for myself occasionally.

"You're right."

"I know I am," I said, trying to sound tough.

"Listen, why don't you come to a party with me some night this week?"

*Seriously? This was his idea of winning me back?*

"I have school, Devan," I said rudely.

"You can go home late one night. I used to do it all the time in high school. Your mom's not even home." Right, my mom wasn't home. But Danielle, who at times could be a monster, was.

"My sister's not as nice as she looks. She's a lawyer, remember?"

"I think you can take her," he said, laughing. He was right. I could handle Danielle. I knew how to break out the blackmail. Right when she started talking about how I shouldn't drink, smoke, and come home late, I'd pull out my trick: "I know what you did in high school." She tried to pretend like it didn't work, but it totally did.

"Okay. One night this week." We hung up after a bit more meaningless conversation, and before I knew it, I was drifting off to sleep with puffy eyes, a bloated stomach, and a new scar on my leg.

\*\*\*

At school on Monday, I was pretty freaked out. Not only did I have a quiz in both algebra and chemistry but a test in my English class about *Romeo and Juliet*. I hadn't studied for anything, to be honest, because I didn't give two shits. Everyone knew senior year didn't matter to colleges. All I had to do was get Bs in my classes and pass the AP psych test at the end of the year.

But for some reason, luck was on my side. In algebra, there was a substitute teacher who didn't give out the quiz. It would be given next class when our teacher was back. Then, in chemistry, the quiz was actually on what I'd paid attention to in class. I knew most of the answers, and for the few I didn't know, I looked over to Luke, the boy sitting next to me. He was smart. He was geeky. He thought I was cute. Needless to say, he let me cheat off him.

I headed into English excited and took my seat. I looked over my notes. I hadn't paid any attention at all in class so far this year, and I hoped it wasn't going to affect my test grade. I still knew *Romeo and Juliet* backward and forward; I just wasn't sure if Ms.

Mallino was going to try and trick me.

"Okay, everyone!" Ms. Mallino said as she entered the classroom late. She was holding a large stack of papers. She walked to her desk, put some papers down, and held the rest.

"We're going to move seats; I have a new seating chart. Then, we'll take our test." Everyone groaned, realizing we weren't going to be sitting next to anyone we knew.

"Billy, Ana, Taryn, Janine, Bobby." The list went on and on, and then I heard my name. I sat down where I was told, right in the center of the room, between a girl who I knew pretty well and, to my right, you guessed it—Andrew.

I looked over at him and smiled. He looked amused by the whole situation. Ms. Mallino handed him a stack of tests, and he took one and passed it over to me with a wide grin.

"Okay, you may begin your tests," Ms. Mallino said with her all-too-cheerful voice.

The test was really, really easy. I couldn't believe how easy, actually. It was all matching and multiple choice, and there were only two fill-in-the-blanks. If I hadn't gotten a hundred, it was a ninety-nine. I was almost positive I'd done well as I handed in my test and sat back down at my desk to read. I was reading yet another Nora Roberts book.

Within fifteen minutes, the whole class was done and buzzing. Everyone was chatting, except me. I really liked the book, and I wanted to finish. I started a new page excitedly, and suddenly it was ripped from my hands.

"Hey!" I said, pretty loudly. Everyone turned to look at Andrew and me. His face flushed just for a second, but then he went on with his business and so did everyone else. He looked at my book, examining it, the page I was on, and then reading the back cover.

"Can I have my book back?"

Before I knew what he was doing, he was writing on the cover. Then the bell rang, and he gave my book back. Everyone cleared out, along with me, as I headed to my locker.

Once there, I opened my locker, exchanged my textbooks and notebooks, and looked to see what Andrew had written in my book. Inside, I found his phone number and a small note.

`Text me, Juliet.`

I squealed to myself and then showed it to Clare, who'd walked over. I was so excited. Beautiful, sexy, cool Andrew wanted me. What the fuck was he thinking?

# Chapter Eleven

By the time I finished my homework and learned a new song for my band meeting on Wednesday, it was around nine o'clock. I was, surprisingly, not tired and still had a lot of energy. This was totally not me. I was the kind of girl that went to sleep at eight o'clock on school nights. I needed ten hours or my whole day was ruined.

I looked over at my phone as it vibrated. One of my guy friends since middle school had texted me. We talked occasionally and it was usually when he was horny or when I needed weed. His name was Liam Graham. We'd been friends for a really long time (even when I was fat), and there'd always been some sexual tension between us. Plus, he was a drug dealer now, and his weed was always fantastic.

    Liam: Hey you
    Stacey: Hey! Miss you :) I wish we had some classes together
    Liam: Me too, why don't you come over? We haven't hung out in a while. I have pot brownies :)

I weighed my options. To see Liam or not to see him. Liam was a cool kid and I was definitely attracted to him, but I knew that nothing would come from our hookup. It was very clear why he was texting me; I was a booty call. If we hung out tonight, we would probably be getting high and hooking up. And that sounded a lot better than option two: sitting in my room alone.

    Stacey: I'm leaving now

I went upstairs quickly, changed my sweatpants to jeans, and put on a bra. I brushed my hair and put a little more blush on my pale skin. I wanted to look hot for him tonight. I wanted him to want me.

I checked my phone.

Liam: Can't wait

Danielle was asleep and would never let me leave if I asked, so I just left. I grabbed the keys and got into my car. I closed the door softly, hoping Danielle wouldn't hear. I turned the car on and slowly backed out of the driveway.

I was a bit nervous about sneaking out. I wasn't into lying to my sister. But part of me knew she would never know, and what she didn't know wouldn't hurt her.

I got to Liam's house on the other side of town in fifteen minutes. It was a small house, being that his mom was a single parent. It was cute inside, though, and it felt very homey.

I texted Liam from my car, and he came outside within a minute or so. I got out of the car and softly shut my door. I wasn't sure if his mom was home asleep.

"Hey," I said, as his arms came around me.

"Hey, I'm so glad you're here." Liam held me, brushing my hair with his fingers. In his arms, everything on my mind seemed to ease. I wasn't thinking about Mike, my weight, or even my sister noticing I had snuck out. Liam was the only thing on my mind.

"Is your mom home?" I whispered as we walked

toward the door. He nodded and put his index finger to his lips, meaning, "Shush." He took my hand, and we tiptoed through the tidy living room, kitchen, and down the hallway, past his mom's room. He opened a door for me slowly, and of course, it creaked.

It was a typical guy's room. There were CDs, clothes, and shit everywhere. As I looked around, he took out the brownies. He handed me one, and I started chowing down. I held my nose as I swallowed the brownie, still tasting the pungent weed in every chew. It. Was. So. Gross. But, I needed to be high.

His bed was the sole spot that didn't have anything on it, besides a rolled-up blanket and four pillows. Being that it was the clean spot, I decided to sit on it. I slid off my flip-flops, put my feet up, and rested my head on a pillow.

"Comfy?" he asked, taking the spot next to me. His hands came to my waist, and he positioned me so that I was holding on to his torso. I was holding him, and my head was on his chest. He was so warm.

"More comfy, now," I said, looking up at him. He was staring at me with his big green eyes. There were really beautiful. Well, *he* was beautiful, to be honest. He had a strong face, a strong body, but at times like this, he showed me that he was still a teddy bear. Any guy who liked when a girl cuddled with him was a softy.

"A lot has been going on with me lately, Liam," I spoke into his chest, trying not to cry. His hand came to my chin and lifted it so that our eyes met.

"Like what?" His eyes were on mine, and I felt so close to him. But I wanted to be closer. I slowly positioned myself so that I was above him. I was on all fours, and my lips were right above his. He looked surprised but definitely happy. He wanted this, and so did I.

His arm came to my neck and urged my head down to his lips. The kiss was so soft, so sexy, so exhilarating. It went on for a really long time. First it was just lips and then his tongue was in my mouth, exploring my teeth, my gums, and my tongue, of course.

I groaned as his tongue touched mine. All I could picture was his tongue and fingers inside me. I wanted that. I wanted him to go down on me. I wanted him to show me how good he was.

Liam's arms came around me and manhandled me. He picked me up and set me down on the bed so he was on top. He took his shirt off and then went back to kissing me. It was even better now because he was on top. I loved when the guy took control. This way, I didn't know what was coming next. It was all a surprise.

"Stace," Liam said, stripping off my tank top. This was him asking me to unhook my bra. I had no idea why it was so challenging for guys to unhook a bra. It wasn't hard. I obliged, though, sitting up on my elbows, unhooking my bra, and stripping it off.

"Oh my God," he said, and then his lips came down to my breasts. He was killing me; it felt so good. I could feel the wetness between my legs. My heart was pounding.

I closed my eyes and synced into the feelings he was creating for me. I savored his touch and thought it through. I loved it. He was getting me so turned on … just as much as Devan had.

"Liam, please … " I whispered, begging for him to stop. I was getting that feeling again. I was close to orgasm. My head was rushing, and my body started to quiver. First my legs, then my arms, and I squirmed under him.

"I can't handle this … " I moaned. He looked up at me and smiled. He was obviously proud of himself. He knew he could easily get me off if he really wanted to.

"Please, Stacey." He smiled and kissed me. "Come for me." I shook my head playfully and kissed him back with tongue. I really, really, *really* liked his mouth. And apparently my tits did, too. Obviously, if he almost got me off by just sucking on them. *Why was he so good?*

"Nope," I said.

He kissed all the way down. He unbuttoned my

jeans, and much to his surprise, I wasn't wearing any underwear.

"Damn girl," he whispered, touching me *there*. "You're so soft."

"It's this thing called a wax," I said, laughing. "It does wonders." He wasn't laughing with me, though. He was down. Way down. His lips were on my skin. He was bringing my legs up so they were on his shoulders. His head was between my legs … and then it started.

My eyes rolled back into my head, and I moaned. *Oh my god.*

"Liam … " I whispered, then groaned. He needed to stop. I was so close. So close to orgasm. So close to the unknown.

His head popped up, and he came back up to me, obliging. He kissed me and stripped off his pants. He obviously wanted a blowjob. And I was more than happy to give that to him.

"Stacey, what do you think about having sex?" He still thought I was a virgin. He didn't know Mike had taken that from me. So, I nodded. Liam was making me feel so good, and I wanted to know what it felt like to be with someone who wasn't raping me. I wanted to know if it was as good as people say it is. I wanted to know if it wasn't scary.

"Yes," I moaned as his lips came to mine. "I want

you inside me." He was smiling like a kid in a candy store.

"Thank God," he said, laughing. "I don't think I've ever wanted someone so much. You're so sexy. Don't worry," he added. "I won't hurt you. I'll go slow." He was talking about my virginity. He thought I was going to be tight and he'd have to be careful with me. I didn't think now was the time to ruin the mood and tell him I'd been raped, so I decided to keep going.

His hands came down to his erection … Damn was it long. Eight or nine inches. Every time I saw a guy hard, I was always shocked. How could they walk around with something like that? It was so big, and it had to fit in their jeans. I didn't even get how that was possible.

He ripped open a condom wrapper and took out the condom. I rolled it on, leaving a little bit of space at the top. He definitely liked when I touched him because his eyes instantly closed and he groaned. I loved that I could do this for him.

He got on top. I held on to his shoulders, gripping his skin. I mean, I wasn't a virgin, but I was still scared it would hurt.

"It's going to be okay," he said, kissing me. "I'm going to go in now." I closed my eyes, waiting for him to push through and go inside me. He finally did, and

I groaned; it really hurt. My eyes welled and started tearing. My fingernails dug into Liam's shoulders.

I looked up at him … and suddenly it wasn't him. Liam was now Mike. I saw Mike's face above me, Mike's body over me. It was Mike's dick that was inside me.

I flailed and cried out. "Stop! Don't hurt me! Please stop! Mike! Don't hit me." I was back in that moment with Mike. I was defenseless again. I closed my eyes. I thought maybe if I opened my eyes again I would wake up from this nightmare.

"Stacey, Stacey, Stacey. What's wrong? Talk to me."

I opened my eyes. He was no longer inside me; he was lying beside me on the bed, holding me to his chest. This wasn't Mike anymore; it was Liam. Liam was there … The monster wasn't. I was hysterically sobbing into Liam's chest.

"Baby, you're here now. No one's hurting you." He brushed my hair with his fingers and scratched my back, calming me down.

My mind was definitely starting to cloud at this point, the weed starting to hit my system. I could tell when I was high because my eyes and my mind seemed to pause. I had to think about everything I did, and it was very hard to stay awake. All I wanted to do was fall asleep in Liam's arms, but I needed to talk to him. I hoped that he'd talk to me about Mike, because I wanted the security of a man. A man to tell me he'd keep me safe.

Within fifteen minutes, he had successfully stopped my crying, but he was still staring at me questioningly with his big green eyes. He was really nervous. He was curious. He wanted to know what was going on. "Stacey, tell me what happened."

I decided he deserved to know, and I rehashed everything. I didn't leave anything out. He stared at me, shocked, for a while after I finished the story and just held me.

"Why did you say yes to sex?" he finally asked. His eyes were swimming with tears. My story really had affected him. He felt really sorry for me.

"I wanted to not be scared of it anymore."

"It was too soon, and you should have told me. I thought I hurt you. I was so scared." He kissed me and held me closer to him.

"I'm sorry," I said quietly. He was right. It was way too soon, obviously.

"What happened when I went inside you?" he asked.

"Your face … it morphed into his. I saw him above me."

"I'm not him, Stacey. Look at me. That guy … he doesn't deserve to live. But me, Stacey … I know what you deserve. I'm not even sure I'm that guy. The guy that would treat you with care and respect. I'm not good enough for you, but I'll always be here if you need me."

His lips came down on my forehead softly. For some reason, that small kiss was more intimate than anything we'd done that night. That one kiss made me want to never leave the security of Liam's arms. But, it also scared me. I may have liked the way he touched me, but I knew deep down that Liam wasn't going to date me. He knew he couldn't take me on; I was a project. We were never going to be together. This was just a hookup.

# Chapter Twelve

The following day was awful. I woke up late for school, had only two minutes to get ready before I drove off (it did force me to skip breakfast, though, which was nice), and got my first tardy of the year. I was already a slacker.

The day went by slowly; school was extra grueling. That probably had a lot to do with the fact that I looked like shit. For some reason, when I wore sweats to school, it made my whole day miserable and made me feel depressed. It obviously had a lot to do with the fact that I didn't want anyone to look at me when my hair wasn't done, I didn't have makeup on, and I was wearing a grungy outfit.

Driving home, I couldn't stop thinking about Andrew. Did he like me? Did he think I was pretty? Was he just trying to live the *Romeo & Juliet* fantasy like I was?

I gave in and decided to text him when I got home. Something cute, simple, and sweet.

Walking into my house at around two twenty, I headed right for the fruit bowl. I hadn't eaten anything all day, so I peeled a banana and ate that awfully quickly. I followed the banana with two heaping tablespoons of peanut butter. Protein and fruit. Healthy, but not too many calories.

I took out my homework and my phone. Before work at four o'clock, I had to finish a rough draft of an essay for English and learn ten vocabulary words for my AP psychology class. Plus, I had to run, text Andrew, and make myself something under one hundred calories for dinner. Oh, and I had to call my mother, who had been annoyingly texting me *all day*. Every period. Every hour. Every freaking time I looked at my phone.

I decided I should probably take care of that first. So, I dialed.

"Hello?"

"Mom?"

"You know, Stacey, you should take the time to call or text your mother more often. I hear about your days from your Facebook statuses. That's just embarrassing."

I laughed at my mother's tone. "Sorry, Mom, there's just a lot going on. I miss you, and I love you. I'm really sorry." I figured flattery would get me everywhere.

"Aw, sweetie! I love and miss you too! Your father and I wish you guys were here with us. Kara and Fred missed you." My mom always said that. But really, us moving every time my dad got a new job wasn't cool, and my mom knew it wasn't right to make me move all the time. I really missed my mom and dad when they were away, but I loved my time with my sister. We had fun together, and we bonded. Plus, it did the same for my mom and dad; it gave them alone time.

"Me too, Mom," I said.

"I know you do, Stacey," my mom said. "So, how's everything going?"

"Everything's great. But I have a lot of homework, and I have to run before I go to work. So is it okay if I call you later?" I heard my mom groan.

"Okay, whatever," she said, like a twelve-year-old.

"Okay, Mom, I love you."

"I love you too, baby." We hung up, and then I went on to task number two: text the hot boy.

`Stacey: Hey :) It's Stacey from`

English class. Andrew, right?

I went on to my homework, hoping it would distract me from waiting for Andrew to respond. Maybe he was just playing with me, and he really didn't want to talk to me. Maybe he gave me the wrong number.

Just as I was thinking all of this, my phone buzzed … multiple times.

Devan: Hey, party tonight?
Andrew: Ya, that's me :) I'm glad you texted me, Stacey (or should I call you Juliet?)

My heart and stomach did multiple flips. *Holy fucking shit. Oh my God.* I smiled and squealed, realizing that not only would I be partying tonight with Devan, but Andrew wanted to talk to me! He wasn't kidding! He *totally* liked me. I could tell.

Stacey (to Devan): I have to work tonight :( After?
Stacey (to Andrew): Aw, well I'm glad you gave me your number. And you can call me Juliet if I can call you Romeo ;)

I was now pacing around my house, skipping, jumping, and even humming So This Is Love from *Cinderella*. I was so fucking embarrassing. I decided I should probably save homework for after my half-hour run since I was so excited. That would help get out my energy.

So I changed quickly, put on my sneakers, and got out of the house. I was going at full blast, running to my playlist (and checking my phone every five seconds, of course).

Devan: Yes, after. It starts at 11 anyway

*OMG. Eleven!* I needed to sleep or school tomorrow was going to suck just like today had.

Stacey: How late are you going to keep me up 2nite?
Devan: That depends.
Stacey: On what?
Devan: On how sexy our hookup is

I was still running at this point, bounding down the hill in my neighborhood, keeping real good time. I was going so fast. I was texting Devan back quickly, a huge grin on my face. Just talking about hooking up with him made my body squirm, my cheeks flush, and my pussy clench. Damn, what the fuck was wrong with me?

Andrew: Now, most girls ... I'd tell them to call me Drew or Andrew. But a pretty girl like you? You can call me whatever you would like :) As a matter of fact, Romeo would like to meet you for coffee. Tomorrow before school?

*OMG OMG OMG OMG OMG OMG OMG OMG.* My pace quickened, and I was racing home. I had to get back as quickly as possible. Not only did I have to go home and finish my homework, but I also had to pick out outfits for *two* dates. One tonight, and one tomorrow morning.

I'd have to straighten my hair!

Stacey (to Devan): I think it'll be sexy babe. Don't you worry about that

Stacey (to Andrew): Time and place Romeo :)

\*\*\*

My cup was empty, my dress was tight, and his hands were all over me. Tits, stomach, legs … and he was definitely flirting with what was in between my legs. He was everywhere, and just a tad bit sloppy. I could really tell he was fucked up tonight. He was slurring his words and laughing way too much, and when we were out in the open with his friends, his hands were down my shirt. It wasn't very classy.

I only had a beer because I had driven us to the party. I decided maybe it was my turn, being that he'd always been the designated driver and paid for gas. Fair is fair.

"I have a question," he said. Ever since we'd gotten to the bedroom, he had been stripping off all my clothes, but still talking a hell of a lot. This wasn't like him. I was the talkative one.

"You do?"

"I don't know," he said, pulling me down onto the bed with him. He kissed me quickly and then looked into my eyes. He struggled to get the words out for a while and finally said, "I just feel like sometimes you don't see what other guys see."

"First of all, that isn't a question," I joked. "What don't I see?" I asked, genuinely wanting to know.

"When I look at you—I see a stunning woman. I don't get how you don't see how beautiful you are."

My eyes started to tear, and I brought my lips to his, closing my eyes, breathing him in. It was around one in the morning, and not only was I emotionally drained from lack of sleep and a long day, but I was with Devan, who put my emotions into overdrive. I was tired, sexually charged, and happy all at the same time.

"I think we should talk tonight," he said, holding me to his body. All of our clothes were off, he was hard, and he just wanted to talk?

"About what?" I asked, laughing and kissing him.

"You scare me," he said, pushing my hair out of my eyes. He stared at me, holding my naked body to his.

"I'm sorry."

"Listen, you really need to talk to someone about your problems."

"Devan, it's not as bad as you think it is." I was lying right to his face now, hoping he'd believe me.

"Yes, it is," he said, holding me tighter. His voice was so soothing, so calming. I was trying so hard not to close my eyes.

I guess I had problems … but I didn't really want to admit it. It was normal for teenagers to experiment with things, and maybe I took that too far sometimes, but that wasn't completely out of bounds.

"It's not, Devan. I promise you."

"I'm really worried about you, and I really wish you could understand how much I want you to get better. I know you don't think I care, but I do," he said, kissing my cheeks, rubbing my back, and occasionally copping a feel. I sank into his touch, and his voice became my lullaby. I held on to him, and I fell asleep to the sound of his soft, sweet voice in my ear.

# Chapter Thirteen

*Fuck. Fuck. Fuck.* My alarm was going off for school, and I was still lying beside Devan. Obviously, we had fallen asleep together.

"Oh my God! Devan!" I jumped up, hiding my body from him, hoping to God he couldn't see the new cuts I'd created and how fat I was in the daylight. I threw on my bra and underwear and searched for my phone. I was scrambling, freaking out, as Devan just groaned beside me.

"What time is it?" he asked, his eyes still closed as he clenched the pillow.

"It's six! I have to be at school in an hour ... and I'm pretty sure we're forty-five minutes away."

"Calm down," he groaned.

My phone buzzed as I tugged on my dress. I couldn't believe I was going to go to school like this. I looked like a hooker, my hair was disgusting, and my makeup was running.

**Andrew: Hey, where are you?**

*Oh my god.* I forgot about our breakfast date!

"Shit! I had a date this morning!" I walked over to the bureau mirror and checked my face. I took out the makeup I carried with me and put on concealer. That helped a little.

"You had a date?" Devan looked a tad angry.

"Yes. I had a date, like, right now!"

I took out my phone and dialed Andrew's number.

"Hey, where are you?" Andrew asked, after one ring.

"Okay, I need to apologize. Like a million times." Devan was getting up now. He was slowly putting on his clothes, rubbing his eyes, and trying to wake himself up. He was also scowling over at me like I was an awful person because I was talking to Andrew.

Andrew laughed, but he seemed a little tense. Like he was trying to laugh off his anger.

"Apologize for forgetting about us meeting for

coffee?"

"Yes. And I have a very long explanation that I would like to tell you. I have a band meeting today after school, but after that, I would love to go to dinner. Is that okay? I really can't make it this morning."

"It's okay, Stacey. Tonight sounds fine. What if you call me after your band meeting, and we'll figure something out?" He hung up quickly but sounded much more easygoing. He might have been annoyed, but he definitely didn't hate me.

"Who the fuck was that?" Devan was behind me now, looking down at my phone, looking for the contact name on the screen.

"This kid Andrew, who asked me to go out for coffee this morning. You let me fall asleep and never woke me up." I playfully hit his chest, trying to lighten the mood. Flirting usually worked with him. "That's not very nice. And I'm going to be late for school now."

"Why don't you stay home from school and play hooky with me?" He pulled me down onto the bed so that I was on top of him. He kissed my nose, my cheek, and then my lips.

"Don't tempt me, Devan."

"Why? You've already been out all night, and your sister hasn't even called. She hasn't realized you're gone—"

"Exactly why I shouldn't press my luck!"

"Nope." He kissed me again. This time, it was much longer and there was tongue. There was passion. There was a certain sweetness to it. "Exactly why you should. Luck's obviously on your side. I'll call the school. I sound like an adult."

I laughed, shaking my head. "You're not that much older than me."

"Yes, I am," he said, smiling playfully. "Please stay."

Was it worth it to stay here with Devan? Risk my sister finding out not only that I'd stayed out all night but that I didn't go to school? Risk the school finding out I was skipping? Risk a detention? I didn't do things like this. Or, I used to not do things like this.

"What would we do today?" Almost on cue, my stomach rumbled. I hadn't eaten since four o'clock the previous day before work. I was really hungry.

"Well, first of all, we could eat." He kissed my nose and put his arms around my waist. I loved that when I was lying on top of him, he wasn't struggling. I wasn't too heavy. He could hold my weight, no problem.

"Okay," I finally conceded.

"So, breakfast. And then we can go to the mall or something. Or we could go back to my house. Or, I mean, if you really wanted to, I could take you to breakfast and then you could go to school."

"Let's go to breakfast, and we'll go from there."

"Okay, let's go." He pulled me up out of the bed, and we headed down the stairs. Together. Hand in hand.

\*\*\*

By ten o'clock, I was back in school. Devan and I had eaten a delicious breakfast and had a lot of fun together. Afterward, we'd had a very nice but not too intense make-out session in his bedroom. Then, I'd realized I had to leave and decided to go back to school.

I had missed my history, math, and gym classes … which I didn't care about. I figured I could handle missing just those few classes. I went to chemistry, which sucked, of course. Then I went to English.

"Hey," Andrew said, sitting down next to me. A few kids came in along with him and also took their seats.

"I'm sorry about this morning," I said, putting my notebook and books inside the desk.

"What happened? You said there was a story." He was facing me now, looking at me with his adorable crooked smile. He had on a green beanie, tight black jeans, and an AC/DC T-shirt. Damn, he was cute. He had the rocker swag.

"Do you play an instrument?" I asked without thinking. I caught myself and laughed. "Sorry, I don't know why I asked that."

He laughed and shook his head with a smile. "Yeah. I play piano, guitar, and drums."

"You're a musician," I whispered, thinking to myself, *Oh my God, he's the perfect man.*

"Yes."

"I'm a singer!" I said, pulling my chair closer to him. This was amazing.

"Yeah, I've heard. From what everyone's said, you're really good."

"Thanks," I said, smiling. I couldn't take the compliment, so I changed the subject. "But anyway, I was with this guy last night at a party, and I fell asleep."

"Your parents must have freaked out," he said.

"They're actually not home. My dad works a couple states away. My older sister watches me at home so my mom can go and spend time with my dad while he's away."

"Whoa, that must be hard," he said, frowning. Everyone had that reaction to the way my family worked. Compared to the typical American family, mine was definitely the exception to the rule. But I really didn't think I missed out on much. My family was loving and supportive. So what if I didn't see my parents all the time? When I did, they were awesome, and that's what mattered.

"Families are all different." I smiled. Our knees were touching now. We pulled our chairs as close together as we could.

"They definitely are." He laughed, shaking his head.

The bell rang, and the classroom flooded with people. The rest of the class was seated, ready to go, and Ms. Mallino was in front.

"Hey, guys!" she said. "So let's get started. We're going to play a game since you all have new seats. I want you all to get with a partner and write down five questions. You're going to ask them five things you want to know about them, and they're going to do the same for you because this person will be your partner for the rest of the year. You have ten minutes. Ready, set, go!" Ms. Mallino looked over to me and winked. She then gave us thumbs up. She'd totally planned this. She was, without a doubt, trying to set us up.

When Andrew and I looked over at each other, we were both laughing hysterically.

"She is the most unconventional teacher ever," Andrew said. I agreed, starting to write down my five questions. I wanted to know how he felt! I wanted to know everything. "I'll start," he said, writing on a piece of lined white paper.

"Yeah, sure."

"Why are you so beautiful?" Andrew asked, looking up from his paper, smirking at me.

I playfully hit him on the shoulder and shook my head. "Next question." I was giggling. He really did make me feel carefree.

"Okay, I figured you wouldn't go for that one." His eyes peered up at the right corner of the room as he thought. "Are you dating the guy from last night?"

I honestly didn't even know the answer to that question. Devan was really hot and cold with me. I didn't know what to think. Were we fuck buddies (without the fucking, of course)? Were we friends? Were we lovers?

"I don't think so … "

He looked at me questioningly, eyebrows raised.

"Seriously, I don't. The relationship fucks with my brain."

"I'm confused," he said, shaking his head. "But we'll move on. Have you ever been in love?"

These were not "get to know you" questions … These were 100 percent, without a doubt, "I want to date you" questions. Part of me was a little nervous that he was interested because I was so fucked up. But the other part loved the attention and was definitely flirting back.

"No." But I giggled, wondering.

"You're quite a puzzle, you know that?" He laughed it off, though, not showing his confusion or frustration. "What's your biggest fear?"

"Getting raped again." The words blurted from my mouth before I could stop them. I was like a robot … saying the truth, not using my filter at all.

"Again?" He looked nervous now.

I paused, and my head went down. Maybe if I let him keep talking, he would forget what I'd said. I would just shut up and wait for him to change his mind. Wait for him to segue into a new topic.

"Did you say 'again'?" he asked, his voice softer now. He put his hand on my leg, lovingly. It wasn't sexual at all. It was just a sweet thing to do. He was showing me that he was there for me. He cared. His arm came around me, and I sank into his embrace. My head rested on his shoulder. My body relaxed. My tears started.

He didn't say a word as the tears fell down my cheeks. He just rubbed my back and held on to my shoulders. He knew I was crying. But, since the whole class surrounded us, he didn't draw attention. He just did the best he could to calm me silently and give me time.

"Stacey?Andrew?" Ms. Mallino knelt down on the floor in front of us. She obviously noticed my tears. She looked very nervous. "Why don't you guys go see the school nurse?" She handed me a slip. It read:

**PASS:**

Take the period off, guys. Ms. Mallino.

11:40

She was actually giving Andrew and me a pass to leave.

"Thanks," Andrew said, picking up my purse, handing it to me, and taking my hand. We headed out the door hand in hand, both of us smiling from ear to ear. (Mind you, I was still crying ... but us leaving together from my English class? That really made the tears start to slow.)

"So, where to?" I said, taking my keys out of my purse and shaking them in front of Andrew's face.

He shook his head, smiled, and then pulled out his keys. "I'm the man, here. We take my Mustang. And where we're going is a surprise."

I wiped my eyes free of my final tears and followed him. We headed down the steps and out the double doors of the school. We walked into the senior lot, found his car, and jumped in.

He turned on the ignition, put the car in reverse, and we fled the premises. I felt like I was soaring. Not only was I skipping class (for the second time in one day), but I was doing it with my teacher's permission. Plus, I was in a Mustang with the cutest guy ever. What more could a girl ask for?

# Chapter Fourteen

When I finally got home from spending the day with Andrew, the boys were waiting on my doorstep for band practice. I was around ten minutes late, and for the first time ever, the boys were on time. I was apologizing before the car was even in park.

"Guys, I'm so sorry! Don't hate me!" I screamed, jumping out of my car.

I ran to them, my arms wide open. Derek had me in a hug first, and for some reason, he was really holding on. Like this hug wasn't just a hello, this was totally about something else.

"I talked to that kid," Derek explained.

"And I beat the shit out of that kid," Jeremy said,

smiling triumphantly.

"And I went along for the ride!" Eli joked. Jeremy and Derek both rolled their eyes. "But seriously, I have been thinking about that kid all week. You need to tell Kara and Fred. I know how good your sister is with helping people, and Kara will know what to do. She's a doctor! You can't do this on your own."

I walked to Jeremy now and hugged him hard.

"Thank you. Thank you so much. I love you." He held on, his hands around my waist, and picked me up like I weighed a total of three pounds.

"I can't wait to hear this story about the three of you losers going to talk to him." I was laughing and moved to Eli.

"I love you, Eli," I whispered. "You're right. I'm going to tell Kara and Fred. They'll know what I should do." Eli always seemed to be right about these things. He was always there; he always had the answers.

"I love you more. We'll get through this together, as a team, as a band, as a family."

I let go of him and wiped my eyes. "Don't make me do the ugly cry. I'll hurt you."

I opened the door, and we hauled all the instruments and equipment inside. Within a few minutes, we were all on the floor, just talking. We discussed our upcoming gigs, songs we wanted to play, and songs we wanted to scratch from our set.

"I really want to play Date *Rape* by Sublime," I said. "Please, please, please, please." The guys stared at me, openmouthed. "Oh my God, not because I was raped! Because it's like my favorite song ever." I laughed, trying to lighten their moods. "Chill."

"Oh … " Eli said, shaking his head in confusion. "I love that song. That's a great idea."

We had ten songs for an upcoming gig, but we were still in the process of figuring out the details and the set list. We were putting our ideas on paper, and it looked like this:

### <u>Songs We Know  :)</u>

I Kissed A Girl by Katy Perry
1985 by Bowling for Soup
Check Yes Juliet by We the Kings
Take Me With You by Secondhand Serenade
I Want You Back by Cher Lloyd
Hero/Heroine by Boys Like Girls
The Anthem by Good Charlotte
Like It's Her Birthday by Good Charlotte
That's What You Get by Paramore
Are You Gonna Be My Girl by Jet

## <u>**Songs We Want To Know:**</u>
Animals by Nickelback
Picture by Kid Rock/Sheryl Crow
Just Like You by Three Days Grace
Fuck You by Cee Lo Green
I Love Rock & Roll by Britney Spears
Island by The Starting Line
I Get It by Chevelle
The Way She Feels by Between the Trees
Dude (Looks Like a Lady) by Aerosmith
What Love Really Means by JJ Heller
Lullaby by Nickelback
We Are Never Ever Getting Back Together by Taylor
Swift
Love Bug by Jonas Brothers
Don't Speak by No Doubt
Grenade by Bruno Mars
Misery Business by Paramore
Hit Me With Your Best Shot by Pat Benatar
Hey Jude by The Beatles
I'm Not A Vampire by Falling in Reverse
I'm The Rehab, You're the Drugs by D.R.U.G.S.


"Finally. Done." I rested my hand and then stretched
it out. It was totally cramping up from all that writing.

"We have our work cut out for us," Eli said, looking down. Jeremy started to do the math for how many songs we needed. "If we try for these twenty and it doesn't work out for all of them, that's totally fine. I'd rather go up on stage with more song choices than less, you know? Just in case people want more."

"Right," Jeremy said, laying his head back on the rug. I looked around the circle to find the boys a little apprehensive.

"We have time, guys," I said, trying to calm them. I got up now, realizing I hadn't put any food out for them. "Let's say we only get ten songs down—not a huge deal. I just want the songs we do pick to be polished."

"Exactly," Eli changed his mind, scanning over the songs on the list. "The songs are all pretty easy to learn, I think. We can definitely get these down in time."

"Thank God!" Derek said. "I have football practice, you know."

"WE KNOW!" we all screamed in unison, laughing. That was Derek's excuse for everything. He couldn't come to practice because he had football. He couldn't learn all ten songs in a week because he had football. He was exhausted because he had football.

"Okay, okay, okay. Jesus!" Derek laughed and took a sour cream and onion chip from the bowl that I set down on the table.

"I'm pretty sure I know the lyrics to, like, all of these songs," I said, looking the list over. Although knowing the lyrics wasn't everything, it was definitely a good start. It was a lot easier to fit the pieces of the puzzle together when each of us knew our individual parts backward and forward.

"I know all the bass parts, too," Jeremy said, high-fiving me.

"Great, so Eli and I have to do all the work," Derek said, groaning.

"Shut up, Derek," I said and hugged him from behind as he got up to sit on the couch. "Guess who has to get up on stage and talk to all the people while all you have to do is play your little guitar. And we all know you're most afraid of the crowd out of all of us."

We were all laughing, rehashing our past gigs. For the first three songs, Derek was always shaking because he was so nervous, whereas the rest of us just rolled with it. We were pretty good with crowds.

"Mr. Shakes strikes again," Jeremy said under his breath. "When we first start playing, I'm always more nervous about Derek falling off the stage or bolting the fuck out of there than getting up in front of the crowd."

I was hysterical now, squeezing Derek tighter. He wasn't laughing. "You guys suck."

"You love me," I said and kissed his cheek as I

sat on the couch beside him. I went to grab a chip and decided that wasn't the best idea. Andrew had taken me for ice cream, and I had eaten pancakes with Devan that morning. I was not having the healthiest day. I reluctantly took my hand away.

"I saw that," Eli said, grilling me with his eyes. "Eat the chip."

"Food Nazi," I said, giving it right back to him. "You eat the chip. You're the skinniest one here." He was skinny as a twig. The kid looked like he ate once a week. I looked like I ate five meals a day. Or maybe six, actually.

He stared at me, shocked, trying to think of a comeback but obviously failing. That was one topic that really annoyed me when people brought it up. No one was going to tell me what I should eat. Seriously, it was the only thing I could control. It was the one thing in my life I could handle.

"Whoa, bud," Jeremy said, eating a few chips and signaling for us to calm down. "We should probably tell you what happened with that kid Mike."

Right. The boys still hadn't told me what happened when they saw him. I was anxious to hear what Mike had to say. Did he regret what he had done or was he still the monster I knew?

"Should I tell the story?" Derek asked. His guitar

was in his hands, and he was strumming aimlessly. No matter what Derek did with his guitar, it sounded beautiful. He came up with the best riffs on his own; he was beyond creative.

"Yeah," we all said in unison. Derek was also very good at telling stories.

"I got his number on Facebook. I called him, and I was just going to talk to him, tell him not to hurt you again, but he was a dick. So I found his address, and the three of us went to his house."

I laughed. Jeremy, Derek, and Eli … angry as hell and all piled up in one car. They must have been going crazy. "Oh God," I said, smirking. This was making me feel better.

"So then we went to his house. He's rich, by the way. Then, I knocked on his door because neither of these two pussies had the balls to." I totally believed that.

"Okay, so what happened?"

"Well, he came outside and closed the door behind him. The kid is huge, which made me a little nervous."

"Derek looked like he was going to shit his pants," Jeremy chimed in. Derek scowled at him and kept going.

"Okay, so when Mike came outside, I told him he was an asshole and you didn't deserve what he did to you. For a while, he acted like he didn't know who you were, which pissed me off. But then he told me you were asking for it."

"That's when everything went crazy," Eli cut in.

"Yeah, everything went crazy." Derek's hands flew around as he told the story. "So right when he said you asked for it, I wanted to kill him. So I punched him in the face. One really good punch. He dropped like a fucking rock."

"The kid was such a dweeb," Eli said, smiling.

"So then he comes at me, and he punches me back wicked hard," Derek said. I could totally believe it. Mike wasn't small; he knew how to fight. "And I'm on the ground. That's when Jeremy stepped in."

"Yeah, that's when I stepped in." Jeremy took over now. He was rushing through the words, smiling. He was very proud of himself. "And I punch him like a hundred times and he's on the ground. I get on top of him, and I'm throwing jabs and right hooks like I'm fucking Mike Tyson. Eli pulled me off him after a while because the kid was bleeding." Eli and Jeremy high-fived each other.

"Moral of the story," Derek said, "is that we fucked this kid up. He got what he deserved, and I have a feeling he won't fuck with you again."

"He better not," Eli said. "I love you way too much."

I loved Eli, too. I loved them all. They were like my family. They made feel safe, at home, and loved. They made me feel like their little sister, the girl they'd always fight to protect. I closed my eyes and took a deep breath. I took in the moment. I was here, with my three best guy friends in the whole world.

# Chapter Fifteen

"Oh my God!" I was on a walk with one of my friends from around the neighborhood, Marie. She was one of the sweetest girls I knew, the funniest, and one of the coolest to catch up with. She was a part of Clare and I's group of friends- but we rarely spent one on one time together like this. Every once in a while we'd call each other up and go for a long walk together. It was always fun to talk, and we were burning calories.

"I know, right? But he didn't kiss me." I was telling her all about Andrew and our skipping-class "date."

"It's only a matter of time," she said, smiling at me. "Do you text?"

"Every second of every day." My phone buzzed just as I said that. "Here he is now."

"What'd he say?"

"He's asking what I'm doing."

"Oh, boring," she said, smiling. "What happened to all the amazing texts you used to send me from the hottest guys ever?"

Marie was referring to a few years ago when I'd been on a sexting bender.

"I haven't sexted in months."

"Months?" We were heading home at a moderate pace now; we were sweating, but we weren't out of breath. "I don't believe you."

"You should," I said, then changed the subject. "So, what about you?"

"What about me?" Marie asked with a smirk.

"Boys. Boys. Boys," I said. That was always what I wanted to know about! I didn't care about many other things. "Tell me!"

"You're so pushy." She laughed, playfully hitting me on the shoulder. "I'm not talking to anyone except that loser from Downey." Downey was the all-boys Catholic school a few towns over.

"Oh, God. I thought we said no to the ginger from Downey?"

"I know, I know! We talked about this. He's not a

good idea … " She frowned. "But, I sort of like him!" She was confusing as hell. Liking a boy that fucked with your mind, drove you insane, and treated you poorly? She was turning into me!

"Why? Because he still talks to his ex-girlfriend who lives in freaking Virginia? Or because he bitches about the fact that you want to wait to have sex? Or how about because he plays golf, the lamest sport in the whole world?" She was laughing now, shaking her head. She knew I was right. He was not good for her.

"I know," she said. I stopped walking when I realized that Marie had. I turned around. "It's his eyes and his hair," she gushed, going on and on about how cute he was. How he made her melt.

I laughed, thinking about my redheaded bartender. "Oh, God, you really do sound like me."

"Sorry," she said, as we started walking again.

My phone buzzed again at the same time Marie's did. We both checked our phones. Our texts were from Lindsey, another friend of ours.

Lindsey: Hey guys, bonfire tonight for Cameron's 18th birthday starting at sundown! You guys are welcome to sleep over. My dad won't be home most of the night

Cameron and Lindsey were best friends who fucked on the *reg*. Apparently that gave her permission to throw him a party—even though they weren't together.

I smiled from ear to ear. I couldn't wait. The only thing I had to do was figure out how to sneak out tonight. Marie and I decided to cut the walk short so we could get ready, finish homework, and come up with excuses.

I needed this tonight: drinking, drugs, that amazing, stimulating high. I couldn't wait for sundown.

\*\*\*

By eight thirty, I was at Lindsey's with my sleeping bag, pillow, a change of clothes, and an awesome present for Cameron. I had told Danielle I was staying at Marie's, and Marie had said she was at my house. Marie and I rarely had sleepovers on school nights, but being that it was senior year, her mom and Danielle seemed to let it go. As I headed to Lindsey's, I was sure Danielle would never know the truth.

Everyone at the bonfire had done similar things, saying they were staying at a close friend's house. Lindsey's house was a huge party spot. Her dad always came home late from his girlfriend's house and left early in the morning for work. He rarely cared about people staying over anyway. Of course, he would say something on a school night, but he wouldn't be home early enough to see it. By the time he was home, everyone would be asleep in the basement, and he would never know.

The fact that this party was on a school night made the night just a little more exciting. There was something badass about it, and I had prepared accordingly. Jeremy had given me forty dollars' worth of weed, and it was all going to be smoked tonight. Cameron was going to love me.

"Stacey!" I walked into the house, and the first person I saw was the birthday boy, surrounded by our friends.

"Cam!" I hugged him hard. Then I whispered in his ear because I wasn't sure if Lindsey's father was around, "I got you weed."

His eyes bulged out of his head, and he smiled. "I love you."

"I know, I'm awesome," I said, as Mark, Lindsey, and Cam's very attractive older friend came over. Mark and I were pretty good friends, having gotten to know each other pretty well over the years. I hugged him, and we said our hellos. We saw each other occasionally at parties but less lately because he had been at college. Clearly, he was too cool for the high school parties now that he was at State.

"What's up?" I said, smiling. I couldn't take my eyes off his dark hair, blue eyes, and toned physique. "You look great."

"You too, Stacey."

I headed upstairs to Lindsey's bedroom with Lindsey and found the rest of the girls piled in there. Marie, Katie, and Jen were all sitting on the floor, laughing and eating from a box of Oreos. I really missed Clare when I saw all of the girls on the floor. The group just wasn't the same without her, but she was at theatre rehearsal.

"Hey, girls!"

"Hey, Stacey!" they all said, handing me the box of Oreos. I took one out and ate it, savoring the taste. Calling an Oreo delicious was beyond an understatement. Oreos were like God's gift to all mankind. And fuck it ... I was eating them. Today had been a bad day anyway, food-wise. So, what did it matter? I'd start fresh tomorrow.

"Guess what I brought," I said, looking over at Marie, who already knew.

"Weed," Katie said.

"Marie told us," Jen chimed in.

"Guess what I brought," Katie said, smiling up at me. She was wearing a wicked grin.

"What?" I asked. I hoped it was a drug or alcohol.

"A handle of vodka." *Yes! Exactly what I wanted.*

"How'd everyone get to leave?" I asked around, smiling wide. Everyone explained how they'd lied to their parents, quietly, as if they would somehow hear it.

I grabbed my purse, where my weed was stashed, and ran downstairs and then outside. The girls followed me.

"You're going to have the best birthday ever, dude," I said to Cameron, walking to the firepit. The fire was blazing, and it was definitely dark out now. It was bonfire time! I took the baggy out for Cameron and handed him one of Jeremy's bowls (that he let me borrow) and also one of his bongs. Cam was so happy. I could see it all over his face.

"Who knows how to do this?" I asked, looking at all the boys. One of the boys in the group raised his hand and started packing the weed. The stench was harsh but was definitely getting me excited.

"Where's the alcohol, Katie?" I asked, searching for her in the crowd of people. She came over to me, and under her sweatshirt was the handle. I ran inside, got a tall glass, and poured a small amount of cranberry juice inside. Then I filled the rest with vodka. I took a deep breath and chugged. Then I refilled it and handed the full cup of alcohol to Cameron.

"Chug. Then we'll go for round two, birthday boy. I'm making it my mission to get you trashed tonight." It was senior year. And it was Cameron's eighteenth birthday. We were going all out. It wasn't even a question.

\*\*\*

"Truth or dare, Stacey!" Cameron screamed, slurring his words from across the fire. He was starting to get just a tad bit flirty with me—which seemed to be annoying Lindsey. But, honestly, I couldn't have given two fucks what bothered her. I was having fun tonight.

"How fucking old are you … Twelve?"

"Oh, come on. It's my birthday. Shut up. Truth or dare."

"Truth."

"How many guys have you blown?"

I stared at Cam, shocked. I didn't think he was going to be the guy to call me out for the amount of guys I'd hooked up with, especially in front of all these people. There were about twenty people in the circle, and most of them were sober. They would remember what I said.

"I hate you."

"Answer, or you have to do more shots," Cameron slurred.

I was definitely done drinking. I was starting to feel nauseous, and I was sitting on the grass for a reason. Standing wasn't an option. "Eight."

"Eight! Damn, girl!" Cam said, laughing along with our friends. They were such losers. Is this the only thing they cared about? The amount of guys I got with?

"You're just jealous you've only gotten head, like, twice," I said, laughing. I couldn't stop laughing once I started. I was snorting, hitting my knee, and then fell back onto the grass.

"Hey, are you okay?" Mark approached and lay down next to me. We were, like, two inches from each other.

"I'm freaking great."

He laughed and shook his head. "Seriously, you're looking pretty trashed."

"You're just jealous you're not as much of a lightweight as me and can't get this fucked up this quick."

"True. Why don't we go inside and get you some

water? You're making me a little nervous."

I obliged, stepping over the girls and clung to Mark. His body was the only thing keeping me from falling.

"You can't even walk," Mark said, laughing, putting his arm around my waist to steady me. We walked inside, and he pulled a chair out for me in the kitchen as he got me some water. I didn't sit but tested my walking skills on the way to the living room in search of something comfier. I made it to the couch without falling on my face.

"I can walk!" I said, very proud of myself. Mark came over a second later with a glass of water in his hand. I downed it, realizing just then that I totally had to pee. "So," I said, trying to sound sober. "How's college?" Like most people at Ridgefield High, Mark had moved on to the State College. It was basically a continuation of high school.

"It's great. I love my psychology classes."

"Psych? I've thought about majoring in that," I said. I was still applying undecided, but it was an option. If I was a psych major, maybe I could figure out why I was so fucked up.

"I could see you doing that. You know, we have a lot in common," he said, smiling from ear to ear. "I missed you." He was so close.

"I missed you too!" I said, giggling. I really had.

He was such a sweet, cool guy. We always had fun together.

"No, Stacey," he said, quieter. "I really, really missed you." He moved even closer, his face nearly touching mine. And then he was on top of me, and his lips were coming to mine.

His kisses knocked the breath out of me. It was so sexual, so hot. It made my insides burn, my throat ache, my heart soar. I wanted more of him.

"Let's go upstairs," I said, all too quickly. I really wanted to be alone with him.

We were upstairs within seconds, and before I knew it, we were on the bed. My shirt was off, as was his. His skin was so soft. He wasn't sculpted like the other guys I'd been with, but he was definitely attractive.

"Touch me," I said, unhooking my red bra. He groaned, bringing his lips and hands down to my breasts, and then to my stomach and the buttons of my jeans. Those came off quickly, as did my panties. He was touching me, feeling me, caressing me.

I took control now, getting on top. I pulled down his jeans and his boxers and got right to it. He was already hard. He was already ready for me. He was there … waiting. Waiting for my lips to come around his dick, to make him scream, to bring him to orgasm.

I took a deep breath and took the plunge. I took him

deep. I took him all in. He screamed my name instantly in shock. I wondered if he'd ever had this done to him before. That only made it that much better.

I knew this always got my guys off, but it usually took a few minutes. With Mark, though, it was almost instant—I could feel him pouring into my throat.

"That was amazing, Stacey."

"You haven't in a while, huh?"

"Yeah, not since my girlfriend and I broke up."

I didn't know he was dating. Most people didn't freshman year of college; it was all about partying and one-night stands. "I thought so."

"I know. I came really quickly." His face was beet-red, and he was obviously very embarrassed.

"Mark, don't worry about it. It's better for me that you did. Less work," I said.

He kissed my nose and smoothed my hair out. "You have sex hair."

"You have the 'I just a got a blowjob' grin." We laughed together, him still holding me as I lay on top of him.

"I can't believe that just happened," he said, shaking his head.

"What do you mean?"

"Stacey … You're, well … You're you. Every guy that's ever known you has wanted to fuck you. And I always wanted to be with you. I always had feelings for you, I just didn't know how to tell you because we were always dating other people."

"Well, I'm not taken right now, Mark, but I'm sort of dating a lot of people," I said honestly. I was sort of dating Devan and Andrew. I had gone on dates with Frank a couple times. I had hooked up with Liam and Mark. I didn't know what was going on with me.

"Oh," he said, frowning. He realized we were not going to work.

"Come on, Mark. You're a good guy. Don't waste your time with someone who doesn't know what she wants." Didn't he get that this was supposed to be casual?

"I know," he said, pouting like a child. "We don't make any sense together." He was 100 percent right. We had no future. We had no relationship. We were just friends. And I really liked it that way.

"Friends?" I asked, hoping he would agree. Yes, we'd hooked up, and yes it was good—but we couldn't date because I liked Devan and Andrew. I couldn't handle adding another guy to my list.

# Chapter Sixteen

The next morning, we all left for school really late. We were on a mission: to get to school on time. So speeding was really the only option. Lindsey, Marie, and I were driving everyone who had stayed over the night before to school. In my car, I had Cameron, two of Cameron's friends, and Katie, who were all looking beyond exhausted.

"So what happened last night?" Katie asked. I turned out of the neighborhood and hit the gas.

"Um, nothing," I said, smiling over at Cam. I was pretty sure Mark had told him everything. He was also smiling, even though it was quite obvious that, like the rest of us, he had a hangover and didn't want to be heading to school. We'd all taken Advil the night before and this morning, but it totally hadn't worked. We all were nauseous, had headaches, and were in awful moods.

Cam was sipping his cup of coffee beside me, rubbing his eyes. "I hooked up with Katie," Cam said, whispering over to me.

"YOU DIDN'T!" I screamed. It might have hurt my head, but the scream was necessary. This was huge. Cam and Katie? Really? He was with Lindsey!

"Did you tell her?" Katie asked, slapping Cam from the back seat.

"Um, since when do you keep secrets from me?" I asked Katie, glaring at her in my rearview mirror.

"Sorry," she whispered.

"I won't tell anyone," I promised. I really wasn't going to. I was a full supporter of casual sex— especially because I was hooking up with people too. It made me feel less slutty when other people were doing the things I was. Cam had a thing with Lindsey, and yet he hooked up with Katie. It sounded a lot like myself, except there were fewer boys involved.

"I can't believe this," I said, laughing and making my final turn into school. "Seriously, this is weird."

"The fact that you hooked up with Mark … " Cameron said. As the words came out of his mouth, I wondered if he was saying this because he wanted to get with me too. "What were you thinking? You're way out of his league."

*　*　*

"I'm not trying to upset you or sound like a jerk, but you look pretty awful." Andrew was beside me again today, looking at me with a very questioning expression. He was right. I looked like shit. My hair wasn't brushed. I was wearing Mark's sweatshirt and sweatpants. I had no makeup on. I looked like I'd been through a war. I was embarrassed, and I felt completely despicable. Partying was becoming a part of my daily routine, and that really wasn't who I was. But something about partying and hooking up with guys made me feel better, happier, and alive.

"It's okay, you're right," I said, trying to sound like I didn't mind him telling me I didn't look good … even though I totally, 100 percent did mind.

"What's the story?" he asked, laughing at me. He obviously knew I'd been out the night before.

"I slept at a friend's house last night … after getting plastered."

"Figured," he said, shaking his head.

"What? You don't party?" I said, shocked. He totally looked and acted like he did. I wasn't trying to stereotype, but most musicians smoked weed.

"I smoke weed … " he said.

*I WAS SO RIGHT*. I smiled to myself.

"But I don't really consider that partying."

"I do."

"Why? It makes me mellow. After I smoke, all I want to do is curl up on the couch with a bowl of some kind of food and chill. It doesn't make me want to dance around a crowded house with a bunch of airheads trying to fuck girls. I don't like drinking and smoking together anyway … I buy some chips, some weed, and chill with a few guys in my basement. Nothing crazy."

"I've never really done anything that I've bought … except yesterday, because it was Cameron's birthday. That was his present."

"You were at that fire last night?" he asked. I nodded. "Oh, so you're that kind of girl. You go to parties, and if a guy hands it to you, you do it." I laughed at his accuracy. I mean, the kid was spot on.

"What's wrong with that?" I had a wide grin, waiting for his response. Clearly he wasn't kidding, though. He seemed mad; his demeanor had changed in a second. I suddenly realized being honest with him probably wasn't a good idea.

"A lot of things are wrong with that. If a guy hands something to you, the only reason he's doing it is to get in your pants. And plus, do you realize how easy it is for a guy to slip something in that drink, or lace the joint he hands you?" He was totally giving me advice like this because he knew I was a rape victim.

"You're right. But what if I want him to get in my pants?" I was still trying to keep the conversation light, but this only made Andrew madder.

"I totally have you pegged. You get drunk from a guy's alcohol and high from a guy's weed because when you're fucked up it gives you an excuse to hook up with him." As I paused, waiting for this conversation to come to a close, he groaned. "Why are you this girl?" He was looking at me like a psychiatrist. One eyebrow was raised in question, both of his hands were clasped into a fist on his lap, and he looked calm, cool, and collected.

"I like hooking up with guys; that's why."

"Bull." He saw right through me.

"What does that even mean? You barely know me."

He was shaking his head like I had it all wrong. I was playing this game: Deny. Deny. Deny.

"You're right! I don't know you that well."

That was for damn sure. The fact that he was judging me now was really pissing me off.

"But?" I knew there was a "but" coming.

"But, I know you don't like hooking up with guys. You're sensitive, and your emotions are written all over you."

"Sensitive girls can be good in bed, too."

"Maybe you're right. From what I hear, by the way, you know what you're doing in"—he coughed—"*that* department. But, I know that you don't do those things for your benefit. You can say it all you want. You can pretend you hooked up with that guy last night—yes, I know you hooked up with someone last night—you have sex hair, plus you admitted you hook up with guys when you're fucked up—you can say you wanted to get with him because you wanted to have fun, but we both know there's an underlying issue here that you need to address. And you told me about this issue yesterday. Remember that?"

Just then, Ms. Mallino came bounding through the door with a handful of papers, screaming, "Sorry I'm late!"

We both turned toward the front of the class and away from each other. I looked over at him a few times during Ms. Mallino's lecture … and he didn't look at me once. His face stayed hard as stone.

By the end of class, I was just as angry and fed up as he was. Who was he to tell me what my thoughts and feelings were and what my actions represented? He didn't fucking know me. And honestly, I didn't want him to. He was being a jerk.

"Hey!" I said, racing after him after class. He turned toward me, slowly, in the middle of the hallway. "What the fuck was that about? You don't have any reason to be fucking mad at me."

"You're right," he said. He still looked so pissed off. "But, unlike you, I respect you as a person. Let's face it, you don't respect yourself. I hear stories about you ... 'Stacey Lorenzo, the cutest and sluttiest girl in the senior class.'"

"They called me the cutest?" I asked, blushing.

"Ugh, you make this so difficult! You are fucking gorgeous, Stacey," he said, pushing me up against the wall so people behind us could walk through the hallway. "But you keep going for these awful guys! I know you hooked up with that Liam kid ... and I know what happened that night! He told everyone you were hysterical when he went in. You think these boys you get with are your friends—they're not! All they want is a good hookup with a sexy girl. And, Stacey, you give that to them ... " I figured he was stopping when he took a deep breath, but no ... he was still going. He was still yelling at me in the middle of the hallway, surrounded by half the senior class.

"Shhh … " I hushed him, motioning to the people around us. He couldn't see them because he was facing the classroom. I could see them, though. I could see them all staring at me, watching me, hating me. My eyes teared up as I looked back at Andrew. I wasn't crying because I was afraid … I was crying because I was embarrassed. I had hooked up with Mike, Frank, Devan, Liam, Andrew, and Mark … all in a matter of weeks. I was a disgusting piece of shit, wasn't I?

"Why the fuck are you bringing yourself down to this level?"

Since I couldn't answer his question, I just ran away. I headed toward the ladies' room. I really didn't give a shit that I had class soon. I needed to get out of there … away from all of that. Away from Andrew.

"Stacey?" Inside the girl's bathroom, I sat on the handicapped stall's floor. I cried and ate a granola bar that was in my backpack. I really needed food.

"Stacey? Is that you?" It was Clare … I could tell by her all too familiar "let's calm Stacey down" voice.

"I'm in here," I said, opening the stall for her. Thankfully, we were alone.

"So, I just saw that," she said, holding me. I was sobbing into her chest as she brushed my hair with her fingers.

"How bad did it look?"

"Do you want honesty or a lie?"

"Honesty," I said, sniffling.

"It looked beyond bad. But, on the bright side, I think he loves you." She laughed, rocking me back and forth in her arms.

"Me? He thinks I'm a whore."

"No, he doesn't. He thinks you've been acting like a whore because of everything that happened with Mike … which is probably true. Or, you were always acting like one, but this thing with Mike just made it much worse … " We both laughed hysterically at that. It was true. I had always liked hooking up with guys because it made me feel skinny, but after Mike, it made my sex drive more intense. It made me *need* guys rather than *want* them.

"I love you," I said, squeezing my best friend hard. She wasn't letting go.

"I love you, too," she said, smiling wide. "You know what you need?"

"Besides to get back to class?" I asked, realizing I was missing a lot of classes lately. I didn't want my grades to slip.

"Fuck class," she said firmly. "Tonight there's a party at Dean Chance's. His parents went on vacation."

"Dean Chance? Like, the boy you fucked last year?" I asked, remembering this boy. He was a gorgeous brunette with a banging house.

"It'll be your last hoorah," she said, wiping my eyes with her unpainted nails. Of course they weren't painted … She was basically a high-functioning boy.

"Last hoorah?"

"I have a feeling you're going to be dating this boy soon. That means no more drunken nights followed by drunken hookups."

I groaned. I would miss that. But that didn't matter—I was still pretty sure Andrew hated me. "How about it's the last hoorah because I should stop hooking up with people altogether?" I suggested.

"That's probably a great reason too," she said, nodding. "Get up. Fuck this, we're seniors. We're getting the hell out of here. I need to find an outfit for this party." I laughed, shaking my head. She would look gorgeous in anything … She really didn't need the outfit.

"Mall?" I suggested, excited as hell. I had $150 in my wallet that I could spend.

"Yes, after lunch of course!"

Lunch. I looked down at my body, seeing the big patches of fat on my stomach, legs, and arms. I really didn't want to go to lunch.

"Ugh, lunch? I just had a granola bar!"

She groaned and took my hand. "Shut the fuck up. I don't care if I have to put the fork to your mouth myself, you're eating."

# Chapter Seventeen

Clare and I sat down at the party, looking hot. She was wearing a short purple dress from Charlotte Russe (that I'd picked out for her) and her makeup was all done. I had sat her down in my bathroom for an hour and did both her makeup and hair for her. She needed to look banging tonight, for Dean.

I was wearing a pair of tight black skinny jeans, red stilettos, and a tight, black tank top. My hair was pin-straight. My makeup was intense. I was wearing dark, navy-blue eyeshadow, and my eyes were super smoky. I had on fake eyelashes and bright red lipstick. To make my rocker look even more intense, I was wearing a leather jacket.

On the way there, I'd been sucking down some of my very favorite Absolut Ruby Red. It went down hard when you drank it straight. When I started drinking, I was instantly happy. Because even when I wasn't drunk yet, I was excited for it to happen. And when I was drunk … Well, Stacey Lorenzo turned into the life of the party.

Two shots in, and I was already tipsy because I had drank so much that week. I was ready to talk to all the guys. The music was blaring, and right when Lil Wayne's Every Girl came on, Clare and I were both grinding. Clare was getting low with Dean, who was very sloppy. The boy I was dancing with was Jeff, a guy I'd met at a few parties. He was tall, cute, but nothing special. He was always the first one to make me feel welcome, even at a party like this (where I didn't know anyone).

Jeff's arms were around me, pressing my butt harder into him. I had an ass, and I definitely knew how to work it. I could feel his boner. The fact that he got hard from me made me feel gorgeous. I must have been hot if his body responded that way.

"Do you still sing?" Jeff whispered into my ear. I nodded, smiling. He remembered!

"I have a band. It's going really well." I was screaming because of the music's volume.

After dancing a few more songs with Jeff, we headed outside. It was chilly, but not cold yet. Somewhere around sixty-five degrees with wind, because Dean's house was on the water. The dock was completely empty, so Jeff and I headed there and lay down. Just as we did, my phone buzzed.

Eli: Hey, how are you? Have you talked to Kara and Fred about what happened yet?
Stacey: LOL ahahahahahahahaha LOL
Eli: Are you drunk
Stacey: Not reallllllllllllly
Eli: Where are you?
Stacey: Newport yyy poo
Eli: Newport?
Stacey: Ugh huh
Eli: Dean Chance's?
Stacey: LOL maybeeeesssssss babe
Eli: Ok

"You know, I always thought you were so beautiful," Jeff said, holding my hand and trying to get my attention away from my phone. I took a sip from my cup and gulped down a few shots of vodka.

"Are you drunk?" I asked, laughing. *Me? Beautiful?*

"That's why you're so pretty," Jeff said, moving closer. My teeth started chattering a bit, so he put his arms around my shoulders and held me to him. He was keeping me warm. "You're not cocky. You don't realize how great you are."

"Jeff," I said, giggling and sucking down some more of my drink. "You don't really know me that well."

"I know," he said, smiling. "I don't have to. You're such a great girl. You're just so great, Stacey." Jeff was, without a doubt, drunk. I realized that now.

"How much have you had to drink?"

"Like twelve beers or so," he said with a shrug.

"No wonder … " I said, pressing my body to his. We were now holding each other on our sides, lying face to face. My boobs were pressed up against his chest, and my legs were wrapped around his.

"I really think you should have sex with me tonight," Jeff said, smiling.

I laughed out loud, realizing he wasn't joking. "You want to have sex?"

"Yes," he said, his hands leaving my back and going down to the bottom of my tank top. His cold hands came up my shirt to my boobs. He was playing with my nipples, teasing me. His hands, his fingers, felt like ice. His touch made me moan.

"Cold," I said, shivering.

"I think Dean will let us use one of the bedrooms," he said. He knew I was thinking about having sex with him. Sure, I didn't know Jeff very well. I was tipsy as hell. I was in a bad situation with every guy I was talking to. All of that was true. But, I wanted to get it over with. I needed to rip the Band-Aid off quickly and hopefully painlessly.

We headed inside. More people had come in since we'd left and the music was even louder. Jeff and I walked toward Dean and Clare, who were all over each other. Dean had Clare pinned up against the wall. One of Dean's hands was on Clare's boob, and the other was holding her chin, pulling her lips to his.

"Dean, can we use a bedroom?" Jeff asked. Clare's eyes opened for just a moment, and she eyed me with a smile. She pulled Dean's body off hers and grilled Jeff.

"If she wants to stop—you stop. If I hear anything different, I will rip your balls off. After that, we'll press charges and fuck your ass up. Oh, and no girl will ever want to touch you again. *Capisce*?" Clare said quickly, with a straight face. Then she wrapped her right leg around Dean and started kissing him again. Jeff didn't seem to mind the threat, and he led me upstairs to Dean's brother's room.

"Sorry," I said, laughing at Clare. She really was the

best friend I could ever ask for. I stumbled up the stairs with Jeff, proud of the way I was handling my liquor. I mean, I had gotten drunk many times that week and still I was holding it together. I wasn't puking in the bathroom.

"It's okay," he said, bringing me into the bedroom. His lips were on mine immediately. He was stripping off all of his clothes in the darkness, but I could faintly make out his body. He had a normal, cute body. His penis was pretty amazing, though.

When he was naked, I figured it was my turn. So I started with my jacket, which I stripped off. Then my tank top, jeans, bra, and panties. His smile grew bigger with every layer of clothing that came off. I liked that, loved that, even. I was making him happy just with my naked body.

"Get on top of me … " he said, getting on the bed. I did as I was told, kissing him as I put one leg on either side of his torso. I kissed down his torso until I was going down on him. I was taking him in my mouth, working his dick in ways I knew he enjoyed.

"Oh my God … "

I kept going, focusing on the main goal: getting him super turned on before we had sex.

The door creaked open quickly, and before I knew it, there was a large boy standing in the doorway.

I could barely see his face … but I knew that it was definitely Eli, my drummer.

"Get your hands off her."

"Who the fuck are you?" Jeff was shielding my body, pressing me against his chest.

"Back the fuck away from her." Eli disregarded Jeff's question and stood his ground. I looked over at Eli, shocked, clutching my hands over my boobs.

He was in the room now, handing me my clothes. "Put your clothes on. I'm taking you home."

He was totally looking at me naked, and I noticed by his expression that he was pretending not to like it. He handed me my bra and my shirt, which I put on as he tried to look at the floor. Then I put on my panties and my pants. Followed by my jacket.

"What the fuck?" Jeff said, obviously confused and disoriented.

"Sorry," I said, following Eli out the door. He took my hand and led me downstairs, where I told Clare I was leaving and then went to Eli's car.

"Eli?" I said, trying to understand what had just happened. Eli had come into a room where I was hooking up with someone, made me put my clothes on, and told me to leave. I loved him, but it sort of wasn't cool.

"What?" he said, opening the car door for me. I

stumbled for a second but got inside just fine.

"Why are you doing this?" I asked when he was securely in the car and turning on the ignition.

"Because I love you, and I was really scared that something bad was going to happen to you tonight."

"Something bad?"

"I didn't want something to happen like it did with Mike. You really can't handle that right now. Especially because I know you haven't told anyone about what happened."

"I need more time," I said, wanting to be able to figure out all my problems on my own.

"No, you need help." He sighed.

"I know how much weight you've lost in the … What is it? … Two or three weeks since it happened? I see what you're doing." He had no idea that I threw up, too.

"Eli, back off. You don't eat much either," I said, angry now. I was at this party to have a good time. He didn't have the authority to ruin that fun and start lecturing me.

"I'm skinny. That doesn't mean I don't eat." He pulled away from the house, slowly, driving home. We both sat there, side by side, so angry that we didn't want to talk. But, his soft hand came to meet mine as we got closer to my house. Yes, we were fighting. But, we without a doubt loved each other. What he did was very forward but he loved me and proved that when he came to get me that night. I needed someone that really loved me tonight. Everything was really starting to eat away at me and I didn't want to be alone.

"Can you stay over tonight?" I whispered, breaking the silence between us.

"Do you want me to?" he asked.

"Yes, please." I wanted him to be there for me all night. I needed someone to talk to, to hold me, to comfort me.

By the time we got home, it was late. Danielle was asleep, so I decided not to tell her about Eli. I didn't think she'd care because she thought the band and I had a sibling-like relationship.

"What do you want to do?" Eli asked, sitting down on my living room couch.

"Well, what if I put down the featherbed here, and that way we can stay up and watch TV until we fall asleep?" Eli seemed fine with the idea, so I got the featherbed from the linen closet, some sheets, and a comforter, and then went upstairs to get some pillows and pajamas for the both of us. I got Eli some of my dad's clothes, and I put on my very favorite nightgown. It was short, pink, super cute, and just a tad sexy.

Eli moved the coffee table to the family room, and

we set up the bed in the very center of the room, right smack in front of the TV. He got in first (after changing, of course) and nestled in below the blankets.

"Why are you so quiet?" I asked him as I got into bed. Just as I got in, his arm came around me instinctively, and I put my head on his chest.

"I'm really worried about you, Stacey."

"I know; I can tell," I said. "I've never seen you be so forceful. Breaking up a hookup? That's not you at all. You're the sensitive one. Those jobs are left for Jeremy and Derek."

"They were out," he said with a laugh. "I tried to get them to come with me." In the crook of his arm, I felt so warm, so safe.

"Oh. That explains a lot."

"Stacey, I love you," Eli said, making me wonder if he meant because we were friends, or because he had feelings for me.

"I love you too." I really did mean that.

"You're one of my best friends," he said, looking down at me. I stared into his eyes, waiting for him to kiss me. For some reason, I wanted him to. That could have been the alcohol still in my system, but I really wanted to be touched tonight.

"Kiss me," I whispered. Eli looked more shocked than anything else, so I did it for him. I leaned my body forward and brought my lips all the way to his. I pressed them softly against his. I made the kiss more intense, opening my mouth and coaxing his open so my tongue could explore the contours of his mouth. I pulled his body closer to mine, taking control.

"Stacey," Eli said, groaning. I wondered if he liked this or not. Were we just friends? Was I making a huge mistake right now?

"Is this a bad idea?" I asked, looking into Eli's clouded eyes and confused expression.

"Maybe," Eli said, this time kissing me first. His hands grabbed my ass, pulling my body closer to his. I moved my knee up along his leg until I felt his dick. He was normal-sized, from what I could feel. I wanted to see it. I wanted to touch him with my hands, my mouth.

His hands came underneath my nightgown, and he explored. First my panties (but not touching anything underneath them), then my stomach, and my bra. It was all lace, which I'm sure he liked very much. He took my nightgown off slowly, sweetly, making sure not to make any sudden movements. Everything about this hookup was in those two words. Sweet and soft.

"Please ... " I groaned, wanting him to take off my panties as he grazed the material. I wanted him to touch everything that was underneath. I wanted him to show me he wasn't just my close friend; he was a man.

"Be patient," he said, chuckling to himself. He obliged, though, and gently took off my panties underneath the blanket. His hand came out from underneath the comforter, and he put my panties next to him ... but not before examining them first. I knew he liked it: they were very sexy panties. Small, black, lace. Panties that were meant to be taken off by a man.

It was so hot underneath the blanket now, I pulled it off of us. He examined me in greater detail than when I was with Jeff.

As he looked at me, he got on top so his mouth was just an inch from mine. He kissed me; it was a long, sensual kiss that made my sex muscles contract. I groaned as he unhooked my bra. He was smiling now. It looked like he couldn't even help it.

His hands massaged my breasts with his hands and then he used his tongue and his gentle teeth to play with my nipples. My body screamed as he worked his way farther down my body with his tongue. He made his way to the place I wanted him ... between my legs.

I groaned between clenched teeth as his fingers and tongue came down to my clit. This feeling was amazing, crazy even. I couldn't believe the way Eli was making me feel.

He came up, though, after just a minute or so, and

that's when I started stripping off his clothes. First the T-shirt, then his boxers. His body was so much different than I expected it to be. His body was sexy as hell. He didn't look like a skinny, lanky kid underneath. He looked toned. I touched everywhere on his body, every inch of his build.

He closed his eyes as I got on top now and went down on him. I took him deep until he was groaning for me, groaning for more.

"Stacey," Eli said, pulling at the back of my neck so I would look up at him. "Please, stop. I'm going to come if you keep sucking me that way." I pulled myself up so that I was above his torso, not his dick, and kissed him.

I didn't really want to just end our hookup with a blowjob. I wanted him to be inside me. I wanted Eli. So, I lay down on the featherbed next to him and told him to get on top of me. I was wet as hell from this whole ordeal, so I was pretty sure it wouldn't hurt, that it would help him slide in.

"I want to have sex with you," I said, matter-of-factly. It sounded really weird coming from my lips. Me? Wanting to have sex with my drummer? Eli? What was it with drummers and me? I always thought they were so gorgeous.

Eli kissed me now, not commenting on what he

wanted … At that point, I wasn't really sure if we were even going to be having sex. As he was kissing me, he spread my legs open with his hands. When he got them open as much as he could, Eli was killing me with his hands, his body. I was so close to orgasm. I felt like I was on the edge of a cliff, about to jump. It was invigorating, thrilling, petrifying, all at the same time.

"Eli … " I said softly, as he positioned his body above me. I knew we were going to have sex now, because his dick was outside my opening, positioned for takeoff. He pushed his body forward gently. I clutched the blankets around me as he pushed even farther now. It hurt. It felt like his penis shouldn't be there … like it was way too big for my body.

"Are you okay?" Eli asked, kissing me.

"Are you all the way in?" I gasped, hoping to God he wasn't going to thrust farther inside me. I didn't think I could handle any more.

"Yes," he said, as I held on to his shoulders. My back arched and my mind stirred as he started moving above me. I was groaning, sweating, moving along with him with every thrust, every movement, every caress. My body felt like it was climbing farther up … farther up something that it couldn't get down from. I needed release. I wanted it.

And that's when it happened—and let me tell you

it was better than the way everyone described it. It was an out-of-body experience. My toes curled, my body shook, and I screamed Eli's name. It was amazing … I was feeling something that my body hadn't shown me yet. I was feeling something that I didn't think I could handle, but I without a doubt could. It wasn't a scary feeling like I thought it would be; it was beautiful. It was like my whole body was someone else's. My body had never made me feel this way.

"Stacey … " Eli said, groaning at my orgasm. Just like I always loved when guys got off from me, he obviously loved that I had from him.

My eyes clouded, and then tears welled … I clutched Eli's shoulders as we pushed through our limits and kept moving forward. The thrusting felt better and better as we kept our slow pace. The longer it went on, the more we could feel each other's needs, wants. I realized Eli loved when my back was arched, and I was meeting all of his thrusts because he would shake and quiver when I did so. In turn, when I moved with him, it felt like we were one person. We were in sync.

After a few more minutes, it was happening again. I was at the top of the rollercoaster, where your stomach drops and you're excited and freaked out at the same time. I was there again … and I was screaming my way through it.

My eyes really clouded with tears this time, and Eli clenched up. His body became limp for just a second, he took a deep breath, and he pulled out. He massaged the shaft with slow movements, and within just a few seconds, he was spilling out. It poured down onto my stomach, and he lay down beside me.

I was still crying at this point, wiping my eyes, sniffling and breathing so heavily that I could barely breathe at all.

"Stacey?" Eli asked, kissing me on the cheek. "Are you okay?"

"I'm amazing," I said, hiccupping. "That was just… "

"Beautiful?" he said, with a tear in his eye also.

"Yeah, beautiful."

# Chapter Eighteen

The next morning, I woke up to Eli's body holding mine. It. Was. So. Hot. It felt as if a lead weight was on top of me. I couldn't move, but a part of me didn't want to. The two of us had both had a pretty amazing night, and I was happy as hell. I didn't want my "joy bubble" to be popped.

Eli stirred beside me, noticing my small movements below him.

"Good morning," he said, moving away from me a bit. I turned over so I could see his face. He looked just as cute in the morning.

"Hey … " I said, wondering if I should kiss him or pretend like nothing had happened. Did he regret it?

"Sleeping with you in my arms … " Eli started, and I tensed. Was he going to say it sucked? He hated it? " … was amazing. I fell asleep almost instantly."

"Really?" I asked and kissed him. Now that I knew he liked it, I wasn't going to hold back. Kissing him definitely made me happy.

"Yes," he said, kissing me back as I got on top of him. That's when I heard my sister coming down the stairs. I rolled off him and jumped up. I walked to the kitchen, getting away from Eli so I could tell her more privately why he was here.

"Hey, Danielle," I said, pouring some coffee into a mug. Eli was a big coffee drinker. "Eli, do you want cream? Sugar?"

"Both, please," He said from the family room.

"Eli?" Danielle asked, looking at me with an eyebrow raised.

"Sorry I didn't tell you. Eli came to pick me up at the party I was at last night, and he crashed on the couch watching a movie."

Danielle shrugged, obviously not minding in the least. "Oh, okay. Thanks for picking her up, Eli."

Eli walked into the kitchen. "No problem, Danielle," He said.

"Do you want me to go and get some muffins or donuts for you guys?" Danielle asked.

I totally wanted a muffin, but that was going to be a lot of calories. "Ugh … " I said, but then Eli was beside me, saying, "yes, please."

"Okay, I'll be right back," Danielle said, throwing on a sweatshirt that was hanging from the doorknob and slipping on some flip-flops.

As she walked out the door, Eli's arms were around me. His breath was on my neck, and his lips, too. His touches made my skin tingle. I was groaning as his hands slipped inside my shirt, feeling my breasts.

I wanted to … I really wanted to try again more than anything else. I wanted him to manhandle me, to bring me to orgasm like he had last night. I wanted him to make me feel like a woman.

"Do we have enough time?" I asked, turning around to face him. I stood on my tiptoes now, putting my arms around his neck. I kissed him.

"We do," he said, kissing me back. "Please, baby?"

I laughed, loving that he was begging me to make love to him.

So, I obliged. And I showed him that I wanted to have sex with him by stripping off my clothes. I backed away from him, and my hands came to the bottom of my dress. My bra and underwear were still off from the night before. His eyes gleamed as he stared at my naked body. He focused on just me for a while, taking me all in. It was bright out, which made me pretty nervous. He probably saw my stretch marks and my scars from the cutting. I tried to push that out of my head as he started stripping.

His pants came off, then his boxers, and his shirt.

"Touch me," I said. He closed the space between us, and his lips kissed all over me. He was so hard; I could feel him up against my stomach. It was so amazing that I was turning him on this way. He wanted me. He wanted me now.

His right hand forced me to lean up against the kitchen table, as his left hand came down. He used two fingers to tease my opening and then he went in. I wasn't sure how many girls he'd been with, or if he had been with anyone at all, but it sure seemed like he knew what he was doing.

I was so wet and ready for him to go inside. His hands guided me so that I turned around and he was behind me. He pushed my back down gently so that my stomach was resting on the table. He urged my legs open more, and then he was inside. Like always, it hurt in the beginning. It was a lot to handle when he thrust his dick all the way inside me.

When he was fucking me, I couldn't control the way my body moved. I couldn't control my orgasms. I couldn't control my thoughts. Sex was the most insane pleasure I'd ever felt.

The orgasm was breathtaking. When I screamed, it brought him to life, too. It was like my pleasure directly affected his. He was screaming with me, pushing harder, faster, stronger toward the finish line.

"I'm … " Eli started. I felt wetter, like some sort of liquid was going inside me. Eli wasn't moving behind me at this point, and I was wondering why.

"Damn it!" Eli said, pulling out of me. He did it pretty quickly, so it hurt just a tad. My muscles were so tender.

"What?" I asked, standing up straight now. Had I done something wrong? I heard a small pitter patter on the floor, so I looked down. There were a few drops of a white substance and a long trail of it running down my leg.

Before I could speak, tears were in my eyes. I was hiccupping, shaking, freaking out. I felt like I was in a nightmare.

"Stacey," he said, holding me close. "I'm so sorry. Please, calm down. I didn't realize how quick I was going to come. I should have pulled out … I really couldn't tell when it was going to happen. I'm sorry. I'm still new at this." He was rubbing my back, trying to stop me from crying. After a while, he walked over to the roll of paper towels and cleaned up the cum on my leg. Then he wiped some off the floor. It was still dripping from me. It made me realize just how much cum there was … and it only took one sperm to cause a pregnancy!

"Why don't you go take a shower?" Eli said, picking up our clothes and walking with me up the stairs. He was still trying to get me to stop crying, but it wasn't really working, to be honest. All I could think about was the fact that I could be pregnant. Mike had pulled out, but Eli, someone I trusted just about more than anyone, hadn't. That scared me.

"Baby, calm down," Eli said, turning the shower on for me. I couldn't breathe. I couldn't speak. I couldn't move. All I wanted to do was crawl into bed and die.

"I'm on birth control," I said to Eli. Sure, I took it every day, but it wasn't always at the right time. Plus, I had heard millions of sob stories about girls who were on birth control and thought they were okay, that their boyfriends could come inside, but had gotten pregnant anyway. I felt so nauseated.

"I know," Eli said. He was putting his clothes on now and putting me in the shower. I put one foot on the wall so my legs were wide open and the water was hitting the area I needed it to. I took out the Dove soap and started washing my crotch, wondering if washing it out was actually helping my situation or making it worse. Was it making the cum go farther inside me? Was that possible? Was the water and soap helping the cum leave my vagina or was there nothing I could do?

"Listen," Eli said, "nothing's going to happen. You're pretty good about taking your birth control, aren't you?"

"Yeah," I said. I was *pretty* good about taking it. I wasn't amazing at it, though. I could totally have been better.

"Why don't I go run to the drugstore, and I'll pick up the morning-after pill just in case."

I couldn't even respond. All I could do was cry and think about how much this whole situation sucked.

"Please stop crying, Stacey," Eli said, opening the curtain just a tad and looking at me. He was so worried. I closed my eyes and started shampooing my hair. Eli was still staring at me. I couldn't see him, but I could feel his eyes. "Stacey, last night and this morning … " I waited for him to speak as I rinsed the shampoo off and started applying conditioner. "This was amazing. I have never felt like this before. And I'm sorry this happened, Stacey. I really am. I'm scared, too, but I don't think we have a reason to be."

I took a deep breath, trying to silence my tears. "It was amazing for me, too. You're the first person I've ever had an orgasm with," I said. This was a huge deal.

"You made me feel special, beautiful, and like I was a woman. I owe you so much. But, that being said, this is really scary."

"I'm sorry, Stacey."

I leaned my head out of the shower and kissed Eli. I didn't want to make him feel like this was his fault. I should have told him to use a condom.

"Don't blame yourself," I said. "It takes two to tango." We laughed and kissed again. Every time I was near him that's what I wanted to do. I wanted to kiss him. I wanted him to touch me. I wanted to be with him.

I shut the shower off, and Eli handed me a towel. I wrapped it around myself, brushed my hair through, and we headed out of the bathroom together. He went down the stairs, and I went into my room to change. There, I stopped crying, and I stood calmly. I was happy, actually. Because I knew that when I worked my way downstairs, Eli would be there waiting for me.

# Chapter Nineteen

Sunday morning rolled around accompanied by severe stomach pains from the morning-after pill I had taken. Eli behaved like the perfect gentlemen about the whole situation, asking if I was okay, buying the pill for me, and not allowing me to give him any money. I knew he was doing it that way because he felt guilty.

As I threw my gym clothes on, my phone went off. I looked down … and my jaw dropped. Andrew? Texting me?

Andrew: Hey, can we talk?
Stacey: Umm ...

```
Andrew: I know you hate me. I'm
sorry I did that in front of everyone.
I was angry
    Stacey: That was obvious
    Andrew: I know
```

I waited for him to double-text me because I didn't think he really deserved the response. I mean, the kid was awesome, but he totally had no respect for me if he yelled at me about my private life in front of the whole third floor. Even if I was out of line, he shouldn't have done that.

"Fuck him," I said, walking to my car. *Two hours at the gym … here I come.* As I headed out of my neighborhood, my phone had a seizure. Eight messages… all from Andrew.

```
Andrew: Look, I'm so sorry for what
I did. And I know it was awful… because
I've felt awful since it happened. I
don't know what you want me to do,
though. You flirt with me, and act
like we have something together, but
then I hear all these stories about
you and it annoys the fuck out of me.
I heard that Monday you were with
```

Liam. Tuesday you were with Devan. Wednesday you were with me during the day and God knows what you did with your band at night. Thursday you went to some party at your neighbors. And then Friday I heard you went to a party with some kid Jeff and were hooking up with him until your drummer came and broke it up.

I tried to think about my response, coolly, rationally, without using the words *Fuck off* or *You're a douchebag* or *You don't even know me*. Those were the three things I wanted to say, but I just couldn't.

Stacey: Okay Andrew, what do you want me to say? That didn't happen? It did. And I'm sorry if it hurt you, but it's not your business … and it's definitely not the business of the people who are giving you all of this information. Your friends (who I assume are guys) want to get with me … that's why they know all of this stuff. They're jealous; they tell everyone everything about my life.

Andrew: You're totally right. They're jealous. But what you're doing is wrong … and it's not like you.

Stacey: Since when do you know what I'm like?

Andrew: Ugh … why do you always say things like that? I do know you.

Stacey: Andrew I can't text about this anymore. You're just pissing me off, and I'm driving to the gym. Get off my back for five minutes.

Andrew: Ouch … okay.

Stacey: Sorry

Andrew: It's cool. Why don't we just talk in person

Stacey: I'm at the gym now.

Andrew: Okay, after the gym.

I got out of my car and headed in. I walked to the treadmill holding my stomach. My stomach was still in knots, but I was hoping it was like when I had menstrual cramps—maybe exercise would help. Acknowledging the fact that running could be extra awful today, I groaned while I got onto the machine. I stretched for a while, procrastinating the running part for as long as I possibly could and then turned on the machine.

I started off at a nice, easy pace … It was a jog, but it totally made me sweat. After a few minutes of warm-up, I put the speed up. I was flying now … pushing myself. But the speed turned out to be too high. The pain in my stomach grew, and I slowed the pace to 4.0 (a fast walk). I just couldn't do it today; I needed a break.

On the treadmill, I got a text from my sister Kara.

Kara: Hey Stacey :) Just letting you know that I can come to your gig! Fred can come too.

I smiled wide, super excited to have Kara and Fred there. I didn't see Kara and Fred very often because they were getting their wedding together, they worked constantly, and they didn't live in our town.

Stacey: Really? I'm so excited now. I'll send you the set list!!! I'm so happy that you're going to be there :)
Kara: Us too! I missed you!
Stacey: I missed you too :(
Kara: What's been going on with you?

It was a severe challenge to text and walk on the incline at the same time. It took all my might not to hold on to the machine as I walked up the hill. It was killing my legs. I didn't know how to respond to what she'd asked, because I knew, as my big sister, she wouldn't approve and would tell Fred—who of course would not be happy and give me a very long lecture about "the dangers of sex and drinking."

Stacey: So much
Kara: I hear you! Me too. Work has been insane.

She was a pediatrician who tried to focus on helping underprivileged families. She never turned anyone anyway.

Stacey: Ugh. I'm sorry. Okay, well I'm on the treadmill dying over here so I'll talk to you soon, and if not I'll see you at the gig!
Stacey: Can't wait! Love you
Me: Love you too!

\*\*\*

After the gym, a long shower, and four glasses of water, I was ready. Andrew was picking me up shortly, and I was very excited to see him. Andrew was always looking out for me, and even when he did stupid shit … I knew he was doing it to try to get through to me.

He showed up at the house right on time, and I headed out the door as soon as his Mustang pulled into my driveway.

"You didn't let me walk to your door … " Andrew said, hugging me from the driver's side of the car. The car was sexy.

"My parents and sister aren't home, so it wouldn't matter anyway." We laughed as we headed out of the neighborhood.

"So, where to?" Andrew asked.

"Are we doing lunch?"

"Yeah, I'm so hungry."

"The Diner?"

"Yes, that sounds great."

I smiled at the thought of a nice Caesar salad. It was definitely a lot more calories than I wanted—but it was the best I could do. Plus, I'd worked out despite my stomach pains in the morning. I was treating myself.

By the time we got there, we were holding hands … and asking for a "table for two." I loved going out to lunch or dinner with a guy. It always made me feel so good about myself. On dates, the boy had to like you enough to listen to you, pay for your meal, and spend some quality time with you. Hookups were short, there was barely any talking involved, and they were getting rewarded. A guy had to really like you to take you out on a date.

While looking over the menu, the grilled cheese with French fries was totally speaking to me. I wanted all of those carbohydrates *so badly*. But I didn't want to look like a fatty in front of Andrew. I had to order girl food … and only eat half the food on the plate. He couldn't think I ate a lot because that would confirm the fact that I was fat.

"What can I get for you two?" Our waitress came over with my diet soda and his Sprite, and we ordered our food. I got the Caesar salad; Andrew ordered a chicken quesadilla with extra guacamole.

"So, let's talk everything over," Andrew said, digging right into our very important conversation.

"Okay," I said, putting my thoughts and feelings out there right away. "You were a jerk."

"Yes," he said, laughing. "You're right … " He grasped my hand on top of the table, which made my heart beat super fast. He was rubbing my thumb with his forefinger, which instantly turned me on. Was this gentle touch the same way he would touch me when I was naked?

"Umm ... " I said, trying to think past the hand-holding and get my words together. "So, why did you treat me that way?"

"Because I care about you. And I think you're making a lot of wrong choices and you need help." He cared about me. Did Andrew want to be with me?

"You care about me?" I asked, blushing, wishing his hands were wandering over my body.

"Yes, I care about you a lot more than I thought I could so soon."

"Really?" I said, still questioning him. How could this possibly be true?

"Yes," he said, getting up from his side of the booth and sitting down beside me. He hugged me. My head rested on his shoulder, and I sighed. This really was amazing. "I wish you could believe me. I want you to understand how much of a catch you are."

"Maybe I could understand if you told me why." Was it wrong if I liked hearing his compliments?

"Where do I even start?" Andrew said, laughing, just as our waitress brought over our meal.

"The beginning?" I suggested, smiling and waiting for his response.

"Okay, well, let's start with your eyes, which are gorgeous. There's nothing sexier than a brunette. I love it straight and curly." He was whispering now. "I mean, your body … It's cute, but it's so sexy, too. Your body screams sex. I've wanted to get you out of those clothes since I met you."

"But you didn't … " I said, honestly a little disappointed.

"I didn't. 'Cause I figured a lot of other guys were already doing that."

Ouch. I frowned, realizing just how true that was. He knew how to hit where it hurt. "Oh … "

"It's okay," he said, wrapping his right arm around me, eating his quesadilla with his left. I loved that. I took a few bites of my Caesar salad, full of cheese and croutons, and decided I shouldn't eat the salad.

"Listen, I want to get you naked," he said, rewinding what he said to make it sound a little better. "I'm sorry I said it that way. But I just don't want to be another guy in a long line." That made me think of Eli, and of course, it made me feel guilty.

"The list isn't that long," I said, trying to sound truthful.

"Yes, it is," he said. "Listen, Stacey. You're not the only one who hooks up with people. But nobody hears about what I do. The whole school hears everything you do. And when I have to hear about everything you do during a hookup, I want to kill someone because that guy isn't me."

\*\*\*

About an hour later, we were in his bedroom, looking through his CDs. This kid had fucking amazing taste in music. From Aerosmith to Paramore, he knew what was good. This made me even more turned on by him. If a guy could understand how I felt about an amazing song, he could understand me as a person.

His walls were completely covered in posters. He had Three Days Grace, Hinder, Nickelback, Say Anything, Taking Back Sunday, Paramore, Dispatch, and Fall Out Boy posters, and a total of five guitars.

"Can you play for me?" I asked. He smiled and shrugged. He chose the only acoustic guitar in the room, then took my hand, and led me over to the bed. We both sat down, and he started playing.

Andrew dominated on guitar. His hands were a blur; I sank into the music.

"You are amazing," I said, as he started playing Wonderwall by Oasis. I loved the song, so of course, I started singing. Just as I opened my mouth, he looked over at me. His mouth dropped open in shock. We made music together, and it felt like we had been for years.

We totally made sense together. We had the same style, the same musical taste ... It was so amazing to play with him.

When the song was finished, we were both smiling. We couldn't believe how great everything sounded.

"Wow. Just, wow ... Everyone was right. You have the best voice I've ever heard, like, in my life," Andrew said, putting down his guitar and moving closer to me. His eyes were so beautiful. He was staring at me, looking at me like I was the most breathtaking thing he'd ever seen. Andrew made me feel beautiful, worthy. "Can I kiss you?"

Did he even have to ask? Instead of answering, I pressed my lips to his.

"Baby," Andrew said, as I pushed him down on the bed and climbed on top of him. I took my shirt off, then my bra. His eyes were gleaming as he gazed up to my bare torso. He liked what he saw.

I went to the bottom of his shirt and took it off him, quickly. I kissed his lips and worked my way down his chest. I loved his skin. He was pale like me. I unzipped Andrew's pants and pulled them down. I kissed him as I pulled down his boxers too.

"Stacey ... " Andrew said, as my hands explored him. He was so hard ... and measuring in at around seven inches. My lips came down on him, and I took him deep … getting him super turned on. But a few seconds in, I stopped, because I didn't want him to come from my blowjob.

I wanted him inside me.

Andrew got on top now and took all my clothes off of me. Just as my panties came off, I was ready for him.

"Do you have a condom?" I asked, thinking about what happened with Eli.

"Yes," he said, leaning over to his dresser and slipping one on. "Are you sure you want to?" he asked, obviously worried about being another guy on my list.

"Don't worry. I've only had sex with two people."

"Two?" he repeated, smiling.

"Yes," I said, and then, realizing I forgot about Mike, I added, "Plus the rape." Just as I said it out loud, I wanted to crawl under the bed and never come out. Would he act the way Mike had, or could I trust him?

"Listen, baby," Andrew said, trying to get those thoughts out of my head. "This will be nothing like that. Just focus on us."

Andrew didn't go slowly like Eli did; Andrew knew exactly what he wanted and he took it. Before I could process what was happening, he was pounding his way inside me. It hurt a bit, but not like it had with Eli or Mike. Every time I had sex, the pain seemed to go away just as the pleasure increased.

The feeling was breathtaking, as he started moving above me. The more he moved, the deeper he went inside me, and it made the sensation that much more intense.

"Oh my God … Andrew … " I tried my best to stay contained, but I couldn't hold on anymore. I let go, screaming through the orgasm.

Unlike Eli, Andrew wasn't tentative—he knew exactly what he was doing, and he showed me that over and over and over as he consumed me. The boy was definitely not a virgin, and he sure as hell knew exactly what I could take and what I wanted him to do. There was something beyond sexy about hard, fast, intense fucking. He knew how to push my boundaries and how to make me feel loved all at the same time.

"Baby." Andrew picked me up and flipped me over so I was on my stomach. Andrew was so strong … he could pick me up, change positions with no problem at all. It was so sexy. I loved that he was taking the control. His hands slipped underneath my body and grabbed on to my breast as he kept plunging inside of me. The movement was relentless … and it was driving me crazy.

"Oh my God!" There it was again. This scary, breathless orgasm that I couldn't control.

"Scream for me baby … " Andrew said, taking his hands away from my boobs and bringing them down to my ass.

He squeezed, which made my whole body want to combust. His touch drove me crazy. Andrew screamed just before he stopped moving above me. He pulled out quickly, and I flipped over so we were both staring up at the ceiling.

"That … " Andrew said, breathing heavily. "You are so amazing."

"Why?" I asked, genuinely wondering.

"It's the way you move below me. Most girls just lay there … but you keep up. You moan, and when you orgasm … your eyes gleam. It's just the weirdest thing."

"Weird?" I said, moving my hands down to his dick and slipping off the condom. It was well intact.

"Wrong word … It's sexy. Sexy as anything."

I kissed him. "I want to be with you," I said.

"You *are* with me," he said, laughing.

"I want to be yours. Your girlfriend."

"You do?" he asked, holding me to his body and looking into my eyes.

"Yeah." I was blushing now, hoping he wasn't going to turn me down.

"You know I'd love to be with you. But I don't

know what's going on with other guys. Until I know I'm the only guy in your life … I can't date you."

"I would never cheat on you," I whispered, frowning. My eyes were starting to tear as I realized that he didn't trust me at all. A guy that I had trusted enough to have sex with didn't trust me in the least. I was so disappointed.

"I just don't want you to be confused by what you want, or who you want. I want to be the only guy you ever think about."

I exhaled, and tears filled my eyes. I wanted more from him. I'd put myself out there, and he'd left me hanging.

"Baby, come on. Don't cry." He seemed frustrated, unsure of what to do next. Eventually, his arms came around me and grounded me. I hated how amazing it felt to have his arms around me. It made me feel even more attached when he was holding me that way.

Andrew wasn't gentle like Eli—but he definitely could be. That made my decision all the more challenging … Eli or Andrew? I had no idea what my answer would be. But, one thing was for damn sure— they were complete opposites. I liked them both for completely different reasons.

# Chapter Twenty

On Monday, when I went into work, my main purpose of the night was to talk to Devan. I had to tell him that we were over. That I had two people who I cared about and who cared about me and that he didn't compare to either one of them. I needed to tell him that I was through feeling confused, scared, and upset about him. He wasn't going to add to my problems anymore.

"What's up, Stacey?" Devan asked as I passed him with two full buckets of ice. He took the buckets from me, noticing that I was struggling and smiled. "I got it." I loved when he treated me like a lady.

"Thanks, Dev," I said, wondering if ending things with him was the best idea. Was I making the right decision? Some days he treated me like a princess; other days I wasn't important to him at all. Should I acknowledge our chemistry and take him as he was?

I headed to the bar, following right behind him and waiting for him to empty out the bins. Then I took his arm and led him into the parking lot.

"You know, you're really confusing," I said, smiling. I wasn't doing a very good job of ending it, was I? I was flirting. Totally flirting. I couldn't help it. When I was around him, I wanted to take his clothes off and do the things that I'd done with Andrew and Eli. I wanted him to be inside me.

"Why am I confusing, baby?" he asked, leaning up against me now. He was smiling a playful, crooked smile. Ah, that smile made me want to kiss him.

"Some days we don't talk at all and others you're the perfect gentleman who won't let me do any heavy lifting."

"You're way too small to carry those. Way too heavy for you."

"I'm a big girl," I said, a little too sternly.

His face was inches from mine. He was totally teasing me. My eyes stayed on his lips, praying they would touch mine. I was on my tippy-toes now, trying to close as much of the distance between us as I possibly could.

"I know you are, baby," he said, and then it happened. His lips were on mine, his right hand roughly gripping my hair. His hips pushed forward so I could feel his hard-on. I couldn't help but moan as his tongue slipped inside my mouth. Something came over me, and I couldn't help but beg for more.

"Please," I said, as he started to stop. "Touch me." He was all business when I gave him permission, kissing, touching, feeling my breasts, my ass, my stomach. And it was amazing how turned on I was by just a few seconds of us making out.

"Oh my God," he said. "We need to stop or I'm going to go crazy. I don't want to get fired, either."

"Okay, good idea," I said, stepping back from him, trying to catch my breath. Out of nowhere, he was laughing. First it was a small chuckle, and then it turned into hysterics.

"What?" I asked, laughing along with him. I couldn't help it.

"Feel this," he said. He grabbed my hand and guided it to his pants. He had a pretty insane hard-on. "I can't even pretend anymore. You make me so turned on. You know just what I like."

"That's what I came out here to say! That statement is the perfect example! You're confusing as fuck!" I said, trying to make him understand. It was really hard to be in this situation.

"No, I'm not, baby," he said, pushing up against me again. It was so hard to yell at him when he was flirting with me.

"Do you have feelings for me?" I asked. His expression looked pained; he paused for a long time. "Seriously, you don't even have an answer?" He still wasn't saying anything, so I walked in the direction of the entrance to calm down and to fix my hair.

He caught my arm, telling me to stop. He looked upset. I knew he wasn't trying to upset me. "Stacey …"

"What?" I said rudely.

"I don't think I can give you what you want. Listen, I love spending time with you, but I am not in love with you."

Finally, I had my answer. It was hard to hear, but it was what I needed. Devan just wanted a sexual relationship with me, and I deserved much more than that.

\*\*\*

Work was very slow, and I left a lot earlier than I usually did with money in my pocket. When I got home at seven thirty, I had two texts from my two favorite boys. And both of them referred to me as "baby."

Andrew: Hey baby, what are you doing? Come to a party with me tonight
    Eli: Hey baby, what's up?

I smiled at both of their texts but decided that spending time with them that night wasn't even an option. I had school in the morning, and I didn't want to have a hangover again. I hadn't felt that great since I'd taken the morning-after pill, and I was also pretty upset about Devan. For some reason, ending it with him was really affecting me.

My sister was doing work when I got home, so I was left to fend for myself. I decided I needed to eat, sleep, and take the night off. Also, it was the perfect night to catch up on schoolwork. I headed to the snack cabinet and pulled out a bag of Doritos.

I took the full bag to the couch, got myself a warm blanket, and put on one of my favorite movies. As the coming attractions came on, I texted the boys back and started doing some AP psych work. I texted Andrew first.

Stacey: Hey, sorry I just got home from work and I am way too tired. I have a date with my couch and a love story that I just can't break. Lol

Andrew: I got you. Wish you were here though. This party's really great.

Stacey: Aw well maybe another time

Andrew: Okay, have fun with your couch lol

Stacey: Oh I will

Andrew: Byeeee

Stacey: Have fun. Be safe.

Andrew: Always am safe. Don't worry

Then I texted Eli.

Stacey: Hey just got home from work early so I'm doing homework and watching a movie

Eli: Can I come over and keep you company?

Stacey: I'm sorry, no. I really need time to myself

Eli: You're not with another guy are you?

Stacey: … No?! WTF

Eli: Okay

Stacey: Seriously????

Eli: Sorry. I'm starting to get anxious

Stacey: About what?

Eli: I saw you with the new kid at The Diner. You were holding hands, so don't tell me you're just friends. That's bullshit.

Stacey: I'm sorry

Eli: WOW

Stacey: What?

Eli: I knew it.

Stacey: You knew what? That I was talking to another guy??? Of course I am. You never once made a commitment to me.

Eli: True

Stacey: Don't make me feel guilty. If you want me … tell me. Don't make me feel guilty when it's you who hasn't manned up and asked me out.

Eli: I want to be with you. I want to be your boyfriend. I want to be the boy that protects you and takes you out on Friday nights. You're everything I've ever wanted.

I stared at that text for like five minutes, trying to figure out what to say. I absolutely had feelings for him … but did I want him over Andrew? My anxiety kicked in, and my hand went farther into the Doritos bag. I ate the bag in under three minutes, disregarding my nausea.

"Who do you love?" I asked myself out loud. Both boys had so much to offer. I headed to the cabinet for the second time and took out yet another Doritos bag, and then I got a notebook. I started to write everything out in the form of a pros and cons list.

I kept eating Doritos and stared at my list … trying to figure out who was the better choice. One thing jumping out at me was that Eli was a member of my band, and I wanted to make sure that this didn't affect my band's success. I decided that I should probably invite Eli over, and that would help. We would have a band meeting and ask the guys what they thought. The band's feelings about us was a total deal-breaker, so I asked my sister if they could come over. When she signed off on it, I texted them all.

```
Stacey: Can you come over? I totally
need a band meeting
Eli: Yeah, be there in 30
Jeremy: Ugh totally. Be there soon
Derek: Heading over now beautiful ;)
```

# Chapter Twenty-One

By eight thirty, everyone was at the house. I had some of the leftover Doritos in a bowl on the cocktail table in my family room, along with some sodas and candy. I was so pumped. I needed these boys. It was time to sing and maybe even open up.

Eli and I were sitting next to each other on the couch. We were so close to each other that our legs were touching. Eli actually seemed a little tense; I wasn't sure if he even wanted to be that close to me. He seemed nervous that the guys would know; he didn't want them to freak out. As I continued to watch Eli flinch as the boys tuned their guitars, I said what I needed to.

"We need to talk."

"No we don't," Eli said, fidgeting. His face was beet-red, and his palms were sweating.

"Chill out, would you?" I said, laughing and taking his hand. I tried to help him relax.

"What's going on?" Jeremy asked, still focused on tuning. Derek looked way more nervous than Jeremy did, though.

"Are you guys leaving the band?" Derek asked, panicked.

"No!" Eli and I both screamed.

I paused, took a deep breath (Eli's anxiety was rubbing off on me), and said it.

"We had sex."

I searched the boys' expressions, and each one had a completely different reaction. Jeremy was smiling, Derek looked angry, and Eli looked frightened.

"You had sex with Stacey?" Jeremy asked, rushing over to Eli and high-fiving him. "Whoa, kid. Who knew the virgin would be the one to get with her?"

Eli seemed to calm down a little with that comment and seemed to be less stiff. He squeezed my hand. "Yeah, I don't know how she's still talking to me. Doesn't make a lot of sense." It was like I wasn't even there.

"Nah, dude," Jeremy said, snagging a Dorito.

"You're a good guy. That's why she's with you." I was laughing, so happy that Jeremy was convincing Eli. When I looked over to Derek, though, I wasn't sure what to do. He looked beyond angry. Our football player was in pissed-off mode, and that made me super nervous.

"Derek, are you okay?" I asked.

"Come on, dude," Jeremy said, trying to calm him. "It's no big deal."

Without a word, Derek got up from his spot and headed toward Eli. Instinctively, I sat on top of Eli, hoping to shield him from Derek. I wasn't sure, but Derek looked a little bit like he was going to hit Eli.

"Stacey," Eli said, lifting me off him and seating me next to him on the couch. "You're not supposed to protect me. I'm supposed to protect you, baby." Eli kissed me on the cheek and stood up. Derek's and Eli's noses were inches from each other. Both boys had on their game faces.

"If you hurt her, I will kill you," Derek said, trying to intimidate Eli. But really, for the first time, Eli looked more intimidating than Derek did. Eli was showing me that he would fight for me; I loved that.

"I would never."

"If you do … " Derek said, still in an angry tone.

"If I do, you can kill me." Jeremy and I started

laughing at that, and so did Eli. Within seconds, Derek was joining in. Eli hugged Derek, and Derek hugged him back.

"You guys love each other," I said, getting up and tugging Jeremy up with me. "Group hug!" We all held on to each other, realizing what we had, and how blessed we were to have each other.

\*\*\*

I was in my sister's bed that night by eleven. The band meeting had gone really well, but after singing through every song on our set list, I was absolutely exhausted. I loved singing, but sometimes late-night practices weren't all that fun.

"I miss Mom," I said to Danielle as I got into bed with her.

"Does that mean you're sleeping with me?" She was working on something with a red pen. It looked confusing. Lawyer stuff. Stuff that was way over my head.

"Obviously," I said, smiling. "I just wish everyone would come home."

"Well, a little birdie told me that a certain doctor is

coming home for your gig this weekend."

"Kara told me, smart one. It's not a secret." I laughed and snuggled up in her sheets. Her bed was so warm.

"So what's been going on with you?" she asked, circling something on one of her papers. "We haven't been talking very much. We're both always out when Mom's not here."

"Yeah, I know … " And then, without changing my tone of voice, I added, "Well, I'm in love with two boys. I'm no longer a virgin because of those two boys. And I have no idea which one of them I'm going to choose."

My sister's eyes popped open and looked over to me. "Did you just say … "

"Yes."

"Oh. My. God," my sister squealed.

"What?"

"I just can't believe my baby sister grew up."

"I wish I hadn't," I said honestly. When sex was off the table, life was a cakewalk.

"Well, I'm glad you waited as long as you did," Danielle said, putting her papers away to face me. "Tell me about the boys! Oh, and wait! Get Kara on the phone! She'll want to know too!" I dialed Kara's number and put her on speaker, and I told both of my amazing sisters the dirty details.

\*\*\*

I was fast asleep in Danielle's bed when I got a text at one o'clock in the morning.

    Unknown number: Hey Stacey, it's
    Tanner Smith. I need you to call me
    right away.

Tanner was a boy I'd never talked to but had seen in the hallways many times. He was a good friend of Andrew's.

I got out of bed quietly, hoping not to wake my sister, and headed into the bathroom. I dialed Tanner's number, hit call, and waited for him to pick up.

"Stacey?" Tanner said, finally answering. His voice was shaking. I could hear him hiccupping. Was he crying?

"What's wrong, Tanner?" I paused, realizing the only reason Tanner would ever call me. "What happened?" I asked. I could hear Tanner more vividly now, and I realized that he was definitely crying. I couldn't handle the male cry.

"Andrew got in a car accident on the way home from a party."

Two and two came together in my mind. Andrew had asked me to go to a party just a few hours before.

"And? Is he okay?" I asked, my voice shaking.

"He's in a coma," Tanner said softly. "I think you should come down to the hospital. Things aren't looking good."

"I'll be right there," I said. I hung up the phone and headed into my sister's room. As calmly as I could, I threw on a pair of jeans and brushed my hair, keeping on the State College sweatshirt I'd been sleeping in. I woke up my sister, she got dressed quickly, and we jumped in the car.

## Chapter Twenty-Two

On the day of Andrew's funeral, I spent the whole morning on the floor of my bathroom. I had forced myself to throw up four times, after consuming ten cupcakes. Usually vomiting gave me some type of release, but this time it did nothing to calm my nerves or silence my thoughts. All it did was make me hungry and upset.

"Stacey?" Danielle asked, knocking on the locked bathroom door. "Are you okay in there?"

"I'm fine," I groaned, wishing she would just leave me the fuck alone. I wanted my mommy.

"Okay, well, do you want me to get you some water? Or maybe some food other than cupcakes?

Should I call Clare or the boys in the band?"

"Can you get me cookie dough?" I asked, wanting more food. I was so hungry. Danielle was right; I had eaten a lot of cupcakes, but since I'd thrown it all up … I was back at square one. My stomach felt empty.

"Cookie dough?" she asked, obviously not wanting to give me more sugar.

"Stop being a mom. Cookie dough. I want it."

She paused at the door, obviously thinking about it. Finally, she gave in and headed out.

My phone vibrated, and yet another message pinged on my phone. It wasn't like I was ignoring everyone who had called or texted me, I just didn't want to talk to anyone. The only person I wanted to talk to was Andrew, and I couldn't do that. I looked through my missed alerts and found that I had a bunch of texts and missed calls.

Mom: Are you okay? I love you. I'll be home by tonight.

Clare: Hey sweetie, I love you. I'm working today, but I'll come over before the funeral starts to get you. I figured you'd want to go together. I love you so much baby. I know how much he loved you, too. Everything will get better. Call me. Please, call me.

Eli: Baby, are you okay?
Eli: I'm here if you need me.
Eli: Should I come over?

Jeremy: Dude, I got your back. Call me

Derek: Love you.

Liam: Hey babe, I heard about what happened. I'm here for you. PLEASE CALL ME BACK. You know I'm always going to be here.

Kara: I love you. I'll be home by 10 this morning.

Lindsey: Hey are you okay? Call me.

Cam: Hey I heard about what happened. I'm so sorry.

Marie: Hey, I love you.

Dad: I love you. I wish I could come home to see you, and we could talk about this. Call me if you need me.

Fred: Hey Stacey, call me if you need someone to talk to. Kara and I would love to have you visit if you need to get away

I sent them all the same reply.

Stacey: Thanks for the support guys. I'm fine.

I turned on my iPod, putting on the "Andrew Playlist" I had created the night before. I turned on the shower and stepped in. I washed my body and started to shave my legs. It was Thursday, and it was the first time I had taken a shower since I found out about Andrew. It felt so nice, the hot water flowing down my skin.

As FM Static's Tonight played, I couldn't help but cry. I hadn't cried all that much, actually. For the last few days, I'd stayed in my bedroom and bathroom.

I slept, ate, threw up, and cut. That's it. As my sister headed off to work each day, telling me she wished she had more sick days so she could stay home, I would stay home and I wouldn't leave the house. I didn't even go to the gym.

I'd called my mom saying that I needed her to come home, but that was really the only person I'd talked to. Tanner had called me a few times to see how I was, and he was the only one I answered for. Tanner was going through a hard time too.

"Stacey?" Danielle said, knocking on the door. She was home with my cookie dough. "Your food's in the refrigerator. I also bought you some celery and strawberries because I know you like them. You're going to get sick if you keep eating sugar."

"Thanks," I said through broken sobs. I wiped my eyes, trying to calm myself down. I didn't want to look bad when I saw Andrew for the last time. If I continued to cry, my eyes would be puffy and red. I didn't want that.

I got out of the shower a few minutes later, still crying. After brushing my hair and teeth, I walked into my bedroom with a towel around my body. When I got in the room, there was Eli ... sitting on my bed, holding a bouquet of red roses in his right hand.

When I reached his arms, I let everything go. I

was hysterical, sobbing into his black polo shirt. He dropped the flowers and picked me up in his arms like a baby. He set me down on the bed and got in with me. He stroked my hair as I sobbed. He told me that it was going to be okay.

"Andrew was the other boy I was talking to," I said when my tears stopped falling.

"I know. Everyone knows. I heard you had sex with him." He was still stroking my hair and rubbing my back.

"I did. I'm really sorry," I said. I wasn't sorry I had sex with Andrew. But I was sorry that I had upset Eli.

"It's okay. We weren't dating," he said, kissing my forehead. He looked down at his watch and saw that it was ten thirty. "You should probably get ready," he said, taking in my face, my hair, and the towel around my body. I laughed, shaking my head. He was totally right. I had a lot to do.

I got up and closed my door. I dropped my towel to the floor without hesitation and put on a pair of panties and a bra. Eli was smiling as he watched me get ready. I laughed as he realized just how much he liked looking at me naked.

"Control yourself," I said, as he stared at my breasts.

"Sorry," he said, reaching beside my bed for a

magazine. I took out my homecoming dress, which was black, and put that on, then slipped on my red pumps.

"Do I look okay?" I asked, hoping Andrew would think I looked beautiful.

"Better than okay. You look perfect." He looked back down at the magazine and started flipping pages as I put on makeup and straightened my hair.

\*\*\*

"Andrew wasn't just my best friend," Tanner said, up at the podium. "He was also the sweetest, kindest, most sincere person I've ever known."

At this point, I was sitting between Eli and Clare, bawling my eyes out. We were ten minutes into Tanner's fabulous speech about Andrew. A lot of people had talked about him, and it was really amazing to hear about him. To remember all of the fabulous things about him.

"I also want to say that the night before his death, we had a pretty amazing conversation. We were always talking about our favorite bands or how much we hated senior year … We never really had important conversations. But, lately, he'd been talking to me about someone. This girl that he really cared for." Tanner was searching for me in the crowd. "Stacey, do you want to come up here?"

I looked at Eli and Clare, and they both nodded, urging me to go up to the podium. My legs were shaky, but I tried to channel my inner rock star as I headed up to the front. Everyone was watching me.

When I got there, Tanner's arms were instantly around me. He led me up to the podium and to the microphone.

"I'm sorry … " I paused. "I didn't really prepare anything." I thought for a while, trying to get myself together. I took a deep breath. "I should probably start off by saying that I didn't know Andrew very long, or even well. We met just a few weeks ago, in my English class." I smiled and chuckled to myself, picturing our first day together. Our balcony scene.

"I was staring at him the entire class, and finally my teacher noticed, and she told Andrew and I to recite a scene from the play we were reading. And of course, I was hooked right away, because we were Romeo and Juliet." I smiled down at Ms. Mallino, who was also in tears, in one of the pews. "I was infatuated with him. We started texting, and one day in school we got into an argument. While we were fighting, I realized that he was one of the only people in my life who actually talked to me honestly." I thought back to that day on the third floor, when Andrew told me the truth and actually spoke to me. He didn't shy away from the hard subjects.

"Andrew is one of the only people who actually saw me for what I was. With Andrew, you had to be honest. He forced it out of you. He treated me the way I deserved to be treated, and he acknowledged my problems and my failures. And that's what I'm going to miss most, even though it's what I hated about him when he was here." I breathed … trying not to cry, sensing that it was only a matter of time until I was hysterical in front of everyone at my school. So, I ended it as quickly as I could.

"I really want to apologize to his family." I stared down to his mother, father, and two siblings. "I wish I had more time with him, and I was just a girl he was dating. I have no idea what you all must be going through." I wiped away a tear, and Tanner took my hand, leading me back to Eli.

# Chapter Twenty-Three

When I got home with Clare and Eli, both my sisters, Derek, and Jeremy were there. Derek had brought cookies (that he said his mom made), Jeremy had bought me a teddy bear, and my sisters had made my favorite foods: macaroni and cheese, mashed potatoes, and string beans.

"Thanks, guys," I said, happy that I was no longer crying. I wasn't sure how I was feeling about everything—but I knew I was happy to have everyone with me.

"Are you guys still having the gig on Saturday?" Kara asked the band and I as she dished out the macaroni and cheese from the baking dish. I hadn't even thought about the gig. I totally wanted to have it. I wanted to sing. It would get my mind off the situation.

"Yes," I said, just as all the boys said "no" in unison. They had obviously already discussed it. "What?" I said, looking at all of them.

"I think you need time," Eli said, putting his hand on my leg and squeezing my thigh.

"I need to get my mind off of this situation! Plus, we've been practicing so hard for this. We're doing it," I said, firmly. The boys nodded their heads, going along with it.

We all ate quickly and watched a movie after dinner. I loved that everyone was there for me, showing me just how much they loved me. At the end of the movie, I got a call from my mom who was supposed to be home tonight.

"Hi, Mom."

"Hey, Stacey, are you okay?" she asked.

I responded with my usual, "I'm fine."

"Baby, I am so sorry, but my flight got canceled. I'm flying home in the morning."

"Mom, it's okay. I can't wait to see you." I didn't want to upset her, but it was a total letdown. I wanted my mom home.

"Me too, baby. Me too."

When I got off the phone, I told everyone, and I

couldn't help but start crying. I really needed my mom. I hadn't seen her in so long. Eli took me in his arms and rubbed my back.

"Maybe your sisters will let me stay over tonight," he whispered.

"Yes, we will," Danielle said. She'd overheard. I think she would have done anything to not have me cry anymore. And, of course, right when I knew that Eli was going to be holding me the rest of the night, my tears definitely calmed down.

"Why don't we play a few songs?" Derek asked, sitting down next to me and holding my hand. He couldn't have been more kind.

"Yeah! That'd be great!" Clare said.

So that's exactly what we did. We played five songs, our very favorites, and then everyone headed out except Danielle, Kara, and Eli.

\*\*\*

That night, after taking a long, hot shower, I jumped into bed in my sweatpants and T-shirt. Eli was downstairs with my sisters, watching the end of *American Idol*. It seemed like Eli was getting along with my siblings just as well as he usually did. Eli was a very easy person to get along with. He was a sweet, honest person, and my sisters were great judges of character. So of course they loved him.

In bed, I couldn't help but look at the card Andrew's mother had handed to me. I looked at FM Static's lyrics, from Andrew's very favorite song … and I realized just how fitting these lyrics were to my life, and just how much music helps you in the worst of times. So I decided to write down my feelings. I needed to. I took out a notebook and started writing.

"Hey, baby," Eli said, walking into my bedroom. He was being really sweet, quiet. It seemed like he wasn't trying to make any sudden movements. "What are you doing?" He sat down on the bed next to me.

"I'm just writing some lyrics," I said, reading them over. They were actually pretty good.

"Can I see?"

I handed them over, and after a few seconds, he looked over at me with shock written all over his face. He didn't say a word but hugged me hard. I held on, loving his warm skin enveloping me.

"Can we stay like this forever?" I asked. But I pulled back from his hug and went to my bedroom door. I shut and locked it, and stood in front of the bed. My hands came to the bottom of my shirt and pulled it off swiftly. There was nothing underneath. I tugged off my sweatpants and then ever so slowly glided off my panties.

Eli picked me up and pulled me down to the bed so I was lying down. His clothes were off in seconds, and I touched his erection just as it was free from his boxers. I waited for him to touch me, waited for him to get me aroused so he could go inside of me.

Eli groaned as I straddled him.

"Please," I said, as he teased my opening. He slipped two fingers inside me, massaging parts of me that made me wiggle with joy. I couldn't handle his hands; his caress on my hot, wet skin. When he touched me that way, it was really hard to be patient, so I pushed his hands away and took control. I needed him inside me. I took him in my hands and eased him inside.

As soon as Eli was completely inside me, I started moving my hips. I was a cowgirl, pushing my horse closer and closer to the finish line.

\*\*\*

Afterward, Eli and I were both exhausted. I lay on top of him, buck -naked; I was much too tired to put clothes on. All I could do was think. Think about how happy Eli made me, how great I felt, how much I wanted to be his.

Sex gave me a high. When I was having sex, I felt calm. I didn't think about my weight, my rape, or Andrew's death. But it wasn't just the sex. Specifically with Eli, it felt like he actually cared. He would never hurt me. He would never go too fast or hard. He was worried about me, my pleasure, and my safety.

"I … " I said, finally getting the strength to speak.

"Yeah?" he said, breathing heavily.

"I want to be your girlfriend."

"You do?" Eli instantly popped up. He pulled me up so that my legs were wrapped around his waist and my arms were wrapped around his shoulders. This was the most amazing hug we'd ever shared. Tears welled up in my eyes, and I told him everything I needed to, everything I was feeling.

"You have been there for me like no one else has. You make me happy, you make me feel special, you accept me for the person I am, and you're everything I could have asked for. I would be the luckiest girl in the world if I was yours."

Eli shook his head in disbelief. "Do you see what you look like? That part of you alone is amazing. But you're the whole package. When you're naked, I am instantly hard. You don't even have to touch me." I felt down to his cock, and it was. He wasn't lying. "But you're also so sensitive and caring. You put others before yourself. And every time you sing at practice, it's like I can feel everything you're saying. You mean every word. You're so talented."

I kissed him softly and smiled wide. "You are amazing," I said.

"No, you are." He kissed me again, touching my breasts.

I laughed and groaned as he caressed me. "I'm too tired," I whined.

"Please?" he asked, pushing me down on the bed. "You won't have to do all the work this time."

The thought of him being on top changed my mind. I loved when he was taking control like the man he was. Just the thought of it got me wet, so I opened my legs wide and welcomed him inside me.

"Thanks, baby," Eli said, laughing as I moaned my way through his entrance. "I love how I begged you, and you are more turned on than I am."

I was laughing too, realizing just how much I longed for him inside me. He didn't need to beg. Making love to him wasn't something that I would ever say no to.

## Chapter Twenty-Four

The next day, while lying in bed post-workout, I heard an "I'm home!" from downstairs. I knew it was my mom. I ran downstairs, screamed, and jumped into my mother's arms.

"Stacey! How's my beautiful girl?" my mom said.

"I'm okay. Thank God you're home!" I said between sobs. My mom and I held on to each other for a very long time, saying how much we missed and loved each other, that we never wanted to be apart again.

"How's Daddy?" I asked as we sat down in the family room. On the coffee table, I had a fruit salad and a big pitcher of tea I'd made earlier in the day and had set up for when my mom got home. I put some fruit salad in a bowl for my mom.

"He's good. His classes are going very well."

"Good," I said, wishing my dad was home too. He was always working. "I'm sure he liked having you with him."

"He did," she said, biting into a strawberry. "This is great."

"Thanks," I said, waiting for my mom to ask me about everything. I didn't know if I was ready to talk. The boys had been telling me to talk to my mom for weeks. It was going to be really hard to talk about everything that happened to me, everything I'd done. But I knew today was the day. She was finally home, we were alone, and it had been long enough.

"So what's been going on with you?" she asked, giving me an opening. My eyes welled up, and I started bawling.

"Mom, I need your help ... " I couldn't handle myself. Memories of Mike raping me, throwing up, hooking up with guys, partying, cutting, and Andrew's death flooded my mind. Step by step, I told her. I went through everything, and I told her it was time for me to get some help.

Just like I knew she would, my mom supported everything I said. She held me, she listened, and she knew just what to do. By the end of the day, my mom had made appointments with a psychiatrist and a gynecologist. And for the first time in a long time, I felt like my life was going to change, and maybe even get better.

***

"Are you excited?" Clare asked on the phone. I was getting ready for my gig. Straightening my hair. Doing my makeup. Putting on my gorgeous, black, off-the-shoulder dress. I put Clare on speaker and set the phone down on my bathroom vanity. I focused on my makeup, my smoky, dark eyes.

"I am so excited. I feel a lot better today. I'm ready to do this."

Clare paused for a second. "There's nothing wrong with continuing to grieve."

"I know," I said, realizing that I really was rushing through it. I could take more time, but I wasn't going to miss out on my gig because of what happened. I had put so much time into it, and I deserved to do something that made me happy.

"Good. That's all I needed to say."

"Okay," I said, finishing my face off with a touch

of ruby-red lipstick.

"Stacey! You're going to be late!" Kara screamed from downstairs. I bounded down the stairs with my purse and slipped on my high-heeled leather boots.

"Let's go," I said, just as the back door opened and Fred came inside. I ran to him, loving that he was here to support me. "Thank you for coming!" I said as he held me in his arms. "You're such a good brother."

We all headed out the door. Fred carried my PA amp, Kara carried my microphone, and I carried my stand. The whole family (except Dad, of course) got into the car with big smiles on their faces. We knew the gig was going to go really well, that everything was going to be okay for the next few hours.

When I got in the car, my phone buzzed.

Eli: Hey, did you leave yet?
Stacey: YES! You better not be texting and driving
Eli: Of course not … my mom's driving
Stacey: Can't wait to see you :)
Eli: You have no idea …
Stacey: See you in a half hour!

Then I texted the rest of the band.

```
Stacey: Hey guys! Hope you left!!
Can't wait to see you both :) I have
the set lists BTW
```

And then, finally, my dad.

```
Stacey: Hey Daddy! I miss you and
wish you were here
    Dad: Me too, little one. Me too.
I'll be home quicker than you think.
    Stacey: Okay. :)
```

When I finally got to the venue, I was unbelievably nervous. But I was excited too.

"Oh my God," I said under my breath as I tried to set up my amplifier. It looked like there were over five hundred people surrounding the stage. "You can do this. You can do this. You can do this … " I whispered to myself.

"You're going to be fine," Derek said, placing his amp next to mine. "We got this." Derek, who was trying to keep me sane, was clearly nervous himself. It was written all over his face.

"Yeah," Jeremy said, hearing us from across the stage. "We know this shit like the back of our hands."

Eli was all set up, ready to go. "Can we start now? We're five minutes late," he said, showing us his watch.

"Are you guys all ready?" I asked, singing into my microphone. My reverb was all set, along with my volume. Everything sounded good.

"Warm-up song?" Jeremy asked, smiling. I nodded. To check our sound levels, we did the first verse of We Are the Champions. Once we raised the volume on the bass, we were all in sync.

"Who's excited to hear some music?" I screamed into the microphone, at our fans. The crowd screamed back at us. I repeated myself until they were all screaming at the top of their lungs.

"You guys are ready! We're ready! Let's get this show on the road! We're going to start off with a song for a very special person who, just a few days ago, passed away in a drunk driving accident. This is for him. The song's called Tonight, and it's by FM Static."

By the end of the song, the crowd loved us, and we were totally in the zone. I was singing in front of my friends, my family, and everyone that had ever supported me. The best part was that I felt like Andrew was there, telling me that being with Eli was the right decision and that he was proud of me for opening up to my mom. Andrew was there, cheering me on.

# Epilogue

"Stacey, how are you feeling today?" Cynthia, my psychiatrist, asked me.

"I feel okay," I said, smiling a genuine, real smile. I wasn't faking. I was on medication, I was going to therapy religiously, and I had gained twelve pounds.

"Tell me more." Last night, after a weigh-in conducted by my mother, the only thing I wanted to do was go into the kitchen, eat every calorie I could find, and throw all of it up. I missed the feeling of control I used to have over my life. But I didn't do that—despite the urge to. I walked into my mother's room, told her how I was feeling, and we talked about it. I cried, she listened. And surprisingly, having my mom there helped. I didn't need a blade or my fingers massaging the back of my throat. I just needed a little motivation, and I could figure out a way to cease my negative thoughts.

Just as I started thinking about my old self, tears stung my eyes. Memories flooded my brain. Cynthia told me over and over that talking about it helped me move past it, but sometimes I still felt alone. I wondered if I'd ever be able to wake up and not think about what I'd been through, or wonder why I wasn't thin.

"It's not going to stop immediately or all at once. I can't tell you that it ever will. But, I will tell you that we are going to do everything in our power to make sure your symptoms lessen and you have a happy, healthy life. It's all about continuing to work through your problems in therapy and being able to talk to your friends and me about how you are feeling. That's what you need to do for yourself."

I nodded, agreeing with Cynthia. I couldn't expect all of my problems to go away in a few sessions.

"Let's talk about Mike. How often have you been thinking about the rape?"

I looked down at my journal, which held my thought chart. Every time I thought about the trauma, I wrote it down. His name wasn't even on the page yesterday.

"I didn't at all yesterday." I smiled, proud of myself.

"That's fabulous, Stacey." Cynthia paused. "Did you have sex yesterday, though?" Initially, talking about my sex life with Cynthia was horrifying. It was like talking about it with my mother. But, eventually, I could talk about it. The more Cynthia and I talked, the more we talked about sex. And I realized through our sessions that my sex life said a lot about me. My past was reflected in what I did with all of those boys. Over and over again, I showed that I had no self-esteem. Over and over again, I desperately tried to control my sex life because I hadn't been able to with Mike. Over and over again, I hooked up with guys because I thought that made me an attractive, desirable person.

"No," I said softly. Cynthia and I both knew I thought about the rape more when Eli and I had sex. Yes, sex with Eli was so different than the rape. First of all: with Eli, it was consensual. With Eli, I was loved, appreciated, pleasured. I wasn't put in my place or demeaned. Despite how great it was with Eli, sometimes sex bothered me. The feelings behind the act may have been different, but sometimes, when Eli wasn't in a position where he was looking at me, or when we were rougher, I would freak out, get scared, and a month ago I had hallucinated again.

"Do you think that's why you haven't thought

about him?" Cynthia was totally pushing me, but I rose to the challenge.

"No. He's not worth thinking about."

Cynthia smiled, writing something down in her stupid notebook. "Absolutely. How have you been feeling about Andrew?"

I couldn't help but smile when Andrew Champagne was brought up. "Well, I feel like I'll never really be completely over Andrew. He'll always be a big part of me. I guess it's just frustrating that I'll never know what I would have done with him, what we would have become, or if he would have been a bigger part of my life."

"I understand. Asking yourself 'what if's' will eat away at you if you continue to think that way, though. Andrew's memory should live on in your thoughts, but his memory shouldn't take over your life."

Damn it, I hated her. She knew everything about me. She was a fucking mind reader. She looked at my face, and just as I started to get upset, she continued to talk.

"That being said, everyone grieves differently. I think you have made a tremendous amount of progress. I think I've done my job, and you've done yours. You're gaining weight back, and you look much healthier now. You seem happier, and from what I have heard from your mother, you act that way at home. I'm so proud of you and all that you have done for yourself. I think it's time we start weaning you off the medication."

"Really?" I asked, thrilled. I knew this day would come. I was finally going to be able to do things on my own. I could stop taking medication, and I could eventually stop going to therapy. I would feel normal again.

When I got in the car, I immediately called Eli and told him the big news.

"I'm really proud of you," he said. "I knew you were doing much better. You seem much happier."

"I am happier, and so much of that is because of you, and all that you've done for me."

"You've done a lot for me too," he said. "And I don't want to sound weird, but I know Andrew would be proud of you too. You've been so strong."

I couldn't help but smile at the thought of Andrew up in heaven, looking down on me. I missed him. Every day, I wished he hadn't gone to that party and made the decision to drive drunk. He was such a good person, who the whole world was now missing out on.

"Thank you."

"I love you so much."

"I love you too."

Oh, yeah, I didn't tell you. Eli and I had started saying we loved each other … and yes, we totally meant it. We cared about each other, we had so much fun together, and the sex … was magical. Plus, ever since that little incident, we always wore condoms. So we were being safe. Our relationship was so much better than any guy I'd been with in the past year. With all the other guys, it was just physical, an absolute cry for help. With Eli, I felt something; there was a spark.

I hung up with Eli and started to do something that Cynthia, my psychiatrist, always told me to do. I took out my "therapy journal"—which Clare and I were referring to as the "loony journal." I looked back at the pages filled with negativity. I saw my thoughts, my feelings written down on those pages. And I saw, little by little, my thoughts and feelings turn from despair about my past to faith that my life was going to get better. It may have seemed like a losing battle, but I was winning. Slowly but surely.

For the first time in a while, there were no tears on the page. And what I was writing down wasn't negative or upsetting. I wasn't venting about a close friend passing away. I wasn't venting about being fat. And I wasn't venting about my innocence being forcibly taken away from me.

I thought for a second, getting out my pink, glittery

pen, and I wrote the only thing that popped into my head. Hope. Because, for the first time in a long time, I was hopeful. I was going to survive. I was going to be okay. And maybe, I'd even have a happy life.

I smiled at my notebook, put my sunglasses on, rolled the windows down, and put my car into drive. When I turned on the radio, my favorite song came on, and I sang the whole way home.

# Acknowledgements

When I look back on the process for writing and publishing this novel, I get exhausted just thinking about it. But, despite the blood, sweat, tears, and—at times—panic attacks, I am so blessed to say "my baby" is published. I couldn't have accomplished this task without the amazing support system I have in my life.

I have to start off by talking about the very first person who read the book, Mrs. DT. Mrs. DT was one of my favorite teachers in high school and was much more than a guidance counselor to me. I was a senior in high school, still figuring out how to write, when I handed my novel over to her. She instilled confidence in me and convinced me that I needed to pursue my dreams. Mrs. DT, I want to thank you for taking the time to not only read my work but support me as a person. You gave me the encouragement I needed to put myself out there, and I will never forget that.

The second person I want to thank is Richard DiLallo. Richard, what would I have done without you?

You were my rock through this whole process. Editing my query letter, deciphering emails about agents and publishers, and of course—giving me feedback on my novels. I couldn't have done any of this on my own and without your constant love, guidance, and support.

I also have to thank Julia Coopersmith—a veteran in the business who always took my phone calls, read my emails, and gave me spot on advice about my novel, agents, and publishers. We didn't know each other—I was just a nervous seventeen-year-old calling into your office—but you always took the time to calm me down and give me advice, despite the fact you weren't taking on clients. I am so impressed by you and what you did for me. Thank you.

To Georgia McBride—a woman who read my novel and didn't throw it aside because it was too honest or raw. Thank you for seeing potential in me, for taking my novel despite the fact that I didn't have an agent and that I wasn't even twenty-one.

To my mother, my rock, who is the only person who can really ground me. Thank you for listening to me complain, stress out, and, most often, flip out about what I had to do. You always kept me calm, cool, and collected. Thank you for being there when I was rejected, for telling me that I would make it one day. To my dad, who always showed me how to be a dedicated worker—thank you for instilling that in me. To Vicki and Ali, you guys are my biggest role models. You have always taught me how to strive for what I want, to go for my goals. You guys are everything I want to be. To Scott and David, my amazing brother-in-laws for always keeping me laughing. To my grandparents, both alive and deceased, who always urged me to be the best I could be.

Lauren, thank you for giving me Microsoft Word tips, helping me pick out "hot guy names," reading everything I've ever written, and always being the friend I need you to be. Charles, thank you for always giving me a male opinion. To all of my countless other friends who listened to me, guided me, and read my work: you are all rock stars.

I know there are people in my life who I forgot— and I am going to apologize for that now. I couldn't have done any of this without the people in my life who always told me I could do whatever I set my mind to. Thank you for being there, for keeping me sane, and always making me feel special and loved.

Finally, I want to thank everyone who read Barren for taking the time to read my work. I can't express how much it means to me. If you feel connected to it, please take the time to write a review, rate it, and tell your friends. Also, I would love to hear from you!

Follow me on Twitter and get in touch! Send me a tweet telling me what you thought or DM me! If you feel connected to my novel because you have experienced things that Stacey did—I beg you to speak up. Tell a friend, parent, sibling, or teacher. Anyone that you feel close to. And always remember that you are not alone.

Love,
Elizabeth

## ELIZABETH MICELI

Elizabeth hails from the smallest state in the union with the biggest heart. She started off at The University of Akron and then transferred to the University of Rhode Island. She is a double major in both Psychology and Human Development and Family Studies. Although she loves writing- she also has a passion for helping others which is why she is studying to become a sex therapist/couples counselor. Elizabeth loves spending time with her family and friends, singing with her band, eating everything Italian, and baking cookies. She is "in love with love" which is probably why the driving force in almost everything she writes is romance. When she's not getting lost in her characters she can be found waiting for her prince charming in her North Kingstown, Rhode Island home.

# OTHER SWOON ROMANCE TITLES YOU MIGHT LIKE

THERE WE'LL BE
UP FOR FOREVER
CLASS OF '98

Find more awesome teen romance books at
http://www.myswoonromance.com/

Connect with Swoon Romance online:

Facebook:  www.Facebook.com/swoonromance
Twitter:  https://twitter.com/SwoonRomance
You Tube:  https://www.youtube.com/swoonromance
Instagram:  https://instagram.com/swoonromance/
Request review copies via swoonromancepr@gmail.com

*a novel*

BOOK THREE IN THE TOGETHER SERIES

# THERE WE'LL
## Be

BESTSELLING NEW ADULT AUTHOR
ALLA KAR

She has one day to make him stay.

UP FOR

FOREVER

Heather Young

# CLASS OF '98

Will they get it right this time,
or waste a second chance to fall in love?

# A. L. PLAYER